The Courage of Cat Campbell

By Natasha Lowe

A PAULA WISEMAN BOOK
Simon & Schuster Books for Young Readers
NEW YORK   LONDON   TORONTO   SYDNEY   NEW DELHI

SIMON & SCHUSTER BOOKS FOR YOUNG READERS
An imprint of Simon & Schuster Children's Publishing Division
1230 Avenue of the Americas, New York, New York 10020
This book is a work of fiction. Any references to historical events, real people,
or real places are used fictitiously. Other names, characters, places, and
events are products of the author's imagination, and any resemblance to actual
events or places or persons, living or dead, is entirely coincidental.
SIMON & SCHUSTER BOOKS FOR YOUNG READERS
is a trademark of Simon & Schuster, Inc.
For information about special discounts for bulk purchases, please contact Simon &
Schuster Special Sales at 1-866-506-1949 or business@simonandschuster.com.
The Simon & Schuster Speakers Bureau can bring authors to your live event.
For more information or to book an event, contact the Simon & Schuster Speakers
Bureau at 1-866-248-3049 or visit our website at www.simonspeakers.com.
Design by Chloë Foglia
The text for this book is set in Cochin.
Manufactured in the United States of America
1214 FFG
2 4 6 8 10 9 7 5 3 1
Library of Congress Cataloging-in-Publication Data
Lowe, Natasha.
The courage of Cat Campbell / Natasha Lowe. — First edition.
    pages cm
Companion book to: The power of Poppy Pendle.
Summary: Although her mother, Poppy Pendle, believes magic ruins lives,
eleven-year-old Cat Campbell is a late-blooming witch whose magical
abilities are bursting to be mastered.
ISBN 978-1-4814-1870-6 (hardback) — ISBN 978-1-4814-1872-0 (eBook)
[1. Magic—Fiction. 2. Witches—Fiction. 3. Self-realization—Fiction.
4. Mothers and daughters—Fiction.] I. Title.
PZ7.L9627Co 2015
[Fic]—dc23
2014031618

The Night Before Cat Is Born

THE BABY CLIMBED ONTO THE BROOMSTICK THAT WAS leaning against the kitchen table. Drool dribbled down her chin and she gave a gummy laugh. Then, waving one chubby little hand in the direction of her mother, she flew off through an open window and over the Potts Bottom Canal.

"No!" Poppy screamed, waking with a start. Her face was damp with sweat, and her braid had come unraveled. She clutched at her husband, reaching over the swell of her enormous belly. "Our baby," Poppy gasped, shaking Tristram Campbell awake. "She was running around the bakery waving a magic wand and turning all the customers into chickens."

"Chickens?" Tristram said, patting his wife's belly. He leaned across and switched on the light.

"Wearing nothing but a diaper. On these little plump legs." Poppy grabbed for her husband's hand. "And then she turned you into a giraffe, Tristram, and me into a penguin. It was awful," Poppy sobbed. "I waddled along behind her, but I couldn't move very fast because I was a penguin, you see."

"Oh, I do," Tristram said, giving Poppy's fingers a gentle squeeze.

"Then she ran into the kitchen and started turning all my cupcakes to stone. And the cookies and tarts and éclairs. And right before I woke up, she got on my kitchen broom and flew out the window. Laughing."

"Must have been terrifying," Tristram murmured in his calmest voice. "Penguins and stone cupcakes and babies on broomsticks. But it was just a dream, Poppy, love."

"A nightmare!" Poppy said as her stomach suddenly lurched to the right. "The most terrifying nightmare you could imagine."

"Have a drink of water," Tristram said, reaching for the glass on his nightstand. He held it up for Poppy and she took a few sips. "Look, Poppy. You're just nervous because your due date is tomorrow, and I'm sure that's quite normal. I'm sure a lot of women feel this way. But it will all be all right."

"You don't know that," Poppy said, starting to shake. "What if she inherits my magic gene, Tristram? I couldn't bear it, honestly I couldn't."

"Yes, you could, Poppy. You're the strongest woman I know. And remember, it often skips a generation or two, so it's not very likely. But if she does," Tristram said, "we'll just face it. Together."

"Tristram, magic almost ruined my life. I hate everything about it. And I do not want that for our daughter." The Campbells didn't know for sure whether they were having a girl, but Mrs. Plunket from the post office swore that they were. And since Mrs. Plunket had correctly guessed the sex of all the babies born in the little Yorkshire town of Potts Bottom, Tristram and Poppy were inclined to believe her.

"Look, it's not worth worrying about something that may never happen," Tristram said, giving his wife a reassuring kiss on the cheek, his beard all soft and ticklish. "Now, try to go back to sleep."

"What if I mess this up, Tristram?" Poppy said. "What if I'm a terrible parent and do everything wrong? I'm so scared."

Tristram turned out the light and wrapped his arms around Poppy's belly. It was as warm as a big pan of bread dough. "You will make a wonderful mother," he said. "I have no doubts about that at all."

"I hope you're right," Poppy whispered, feeling her baby shift about as if she was trying to turn a somersault. "I really hope you're right."

Chapter One

....

A Passion for Magic

THE FOLLOWING AFTERNOON AT 3:35, CAT CAMPBELL was born on the floor of her mother's bakery, right into the strong, hairy arms of her father. Tristram had been trying to hustle Poppy, who was clearly in labor, away from the caramel cookies she had been baking and off to the Potts Bottom hospital. But Poppy insisted on getting her last batch of cookies out of the oven first, and so Cat was born on a hot August day, in an even hotter kitchen, greeted by the scent of burning caramel. Her father wrapped Cat up in his none too clean shirt, and she gripped his finger tight in her hand. Staring right at him out of deep green eyes, Cat kicked her spindly legs free. Then, opening her mouth wide, she gave a loud, lusty roar. "Little lion!" Tristram murmured, his fatherly heart bursting with pride.

"Can I hold her?" Poppy said, stretching out her arms. She sighed with happiness as Tristram gently lowered baby Catherine into them. "Oh, she's got your red hair, Tristram! How wonderful."

"And I bet she gets your passion for baking," Tristram said, grinning through his wild, bushy beard. "How could she not, being born in a bakery?"

Cradling her baby close, Poppy whispered, "I don't mind what she does. I really don't. Just so long as it isn't witchcraft."

As Cat grew older she loved to sit on the floor of the bakery, which was also the Campbells' little home, converted from an old, abandoned cottage that sat beside the Potts Bottom Canal. It was a few minutes' walk from the center of town, but nobody minded the detour because Cat's mother made the most delicious breads and pastries. Cat would stir imaginary concoctions around in saucepans, banging on their metal sides and chattering away in baby language. When she was two, Tristram made his daughter a wooden stool so she could stand at the counter mixing up her own special recipes beside her mother and Marie Claire, the elderly Frenchwoman who owned the bakery along with Poppy. Cat liked to raid the spice shelf, shaking cinnamon, ginger, and chili powder into her bowl. She'd open all her mother's canisters, spooning in cornmeal and brown sugar. Anything Cat could wrap her tiny hands around she'd use. One time a ladybug flew onto the table and Cat scooped him up before he could escape, dropping him into her batter.

"Insect cake! Yummy," Cat's dad said, watching Cat stir it around with her spoon.

"Ibeldy gobble," Cat shrieked, jumping up and down and waving the spoon over the bowl.

"A great baker, just like her mother!" Tristram commented. And Poppy couldn't help smiling because Cat did seem so happy in the kitchen, even though her experiments always ended up getting poured down the sink.

"What are you making?" Poppy asked one afternoon, as three-year-old Cat was hard at work. "Is it a lemon cake?"

Cat shook her head, sprinkling pepper and cloves into her bowl.

"How about a chocolate cake?" Marie Claire suggested.

"No," Cat replied, plopping in a spoonful of cocoa.

"Not too much, now," Poppy said, removing the tin

from her daughter's reach. "Cocoa's expensive!" She gave an indulgent shake of her head. "So what are you making, Cat? Cookies?"

"A fly spell," Cat announced. "I want to learn to fly."

"Like an airplane?" Poppy said, a touch nervously.

"Uh-uh." Cat shook her head. "Like a witch, Mamma. I want to be a witch." Cat grabbed the kitchen broom and smeared the sticky potion all over it, and then, with the broom between her legs, she jumped off her little stool.

"That's enough," Poppy snapped, startling Cat as she tugged the broom away. Poppy handed her a wooden spoon instead. "You're making a huge mess. And Marie Claire needs this broom to sweep the floor."

"Mine," Cat cried out, pointing at the broomstick.

"It is not yours," Poppy replied with rather more force than was necessary. Cat's little face started to crumple, unused to hearing her mother sound so sharp.

"Why don't you help me make cookies?" Poppy suggested more gently.

"No." Cat shook her head. "No," she said again, dipping the spoon handle into her bowl of homemade potion. She lifted it out and held it up for Poppy to see. "I fly on this then," Cat declared, straddling the wooden spoon.

Crossing her fingers under the table, Poppy made

a silent plea. *Please, please, please, don't let my daughter be magic,* she begged.

Poppy knew that if a child was going to inherit the magic gene, it usually showed up around four or five years old, so there was plenty of time yet. But although Cat spent every spare minute she had leaping off chairs with her arms outstretched, and mixing up pretend potions, she didn't, much to her mother's relief, show any real signs of magic.

"What are you going to do if she does start casting proper spells?" Tristram said one afternoon as he and Poppy watched Cat through the kitchen window. Their five-year-old daughter wore a witch's hat she had made out of paper and was waving a stick in the air. "It might still happen, Poppy. And you need to be prepared."

"I can't bear to think about such a thing," Poppy said, folding her arms tightly across her chest. "You cannot possibly understand how that makes me feel."

"I think I can understand what it would be like to have a passion you couldn't follow," Tristram said gently. "Imagine how unhappy you'd be if you didn't bake, Poppy. And I'd be miserable if you wanted me to stay home all the time and get a regular job, give up my research." He scratched his compass tattoo and said, "I love discovering new species of plants and exploring different parts of the world."

Poppy sighed, but she didn't reply, and they both watched Cat, who was clearly trying to put a spell on one of the chickens that was pecking around the yard, waving her stick in front of its face. "I love what I do, and you love what you do," Tristram continued, "and right now poor Cat can only pretend. She can't do what she loves. But if the day ever comes when she can, you're going to have to be prepared, Poppy."

"I don't want to talk about this," Poppy said, turning away from the window.

As the years passed by, Cat's passion for magic grew, even though it became clear that she hadn't inherited the magic gene. It was so unfair, Cat thought as she blew out her birthday candles year after year. Her mother was, or had been, a witch long ago—a pretty good one too, according to her grandparents. And yet she had given it all up to become a baker. *A baker!* How boring was that? Standing in a hot kitchen all day, spending hours and hours making things that would disappear in a couple of bites. What a waste of time, when you could buy a perfectly good cake from Super Savers Market. And how wonderful it must have been to be magical. Her grandmother often told her how they had first discovered Poppy had the gift of magic—how when she was a baby she had blown beautiful multicolored bubbles and how, just by waving her baby fists around, wonderful iced cakes would appear. Cat sometimes tried blowing bubbles in front of the mirror, but try as she might, all she managed to produce was a colorless bit of drool down her chin. That's what Cat thought so unfair—her mother had the gift and didn't appreciate it at all, while she, Cat, who really, really wanted it, couldn't even manage a magical dribble.

"Why on earth doesn't Mum just use magic?" Cat would sometimes ask her father, when the bakery had been particularly busy and Cat's mother was exhausted from a day spent baking batch after batch of delicious cakes and cookies.

"Take a look at *The Compendium of Witchcraft Cookery* sometime, Cat," her father would reply with a grin. "You don't want to know what goes into those cookie spells. They say they always use all natural ingredients, but really . . . a smear of snail's slime, a wisp of worm's wind. . . . Let's be thankful Mum likes to do it the hard way. Nothing beats butter." And he'd take another large mouthful of caramel crunch cookie.

"I'd use magic all the time if I had the gift," Cat would say wistfully, waving a wooden spoon around the kitchen. "Abracazam!" she'd cry out, but nothing ever happened.

Most days, after school, Cat loved to watch the Ruthersfield girls come swooping along the canal path on their broomsticks, propping them outside the bakery as casually as if they were umbrellas. They'd swan through the door in their smart purple uniforms, magic wands sticking out of their backpacks. Ruthersfield Academy was the only accredited school for magic in the country, and it was right in the center of Potts Bottom. Cat would have traded her last bag of jelly beans to go there. She'd hear the girls groan about spell tests and potions class as they bought bags of sticky buns, and the longing inside Cat would grow so intense it became almost a physical ache. She had tried talking to her mother about Ruthersfield, about what it was like when she had gone there, but Poppy refused to discuss it at all.

"Magic made me miserable, Cat." That was all she would say.

"But didn't you love flying on a broomstick, Mamma, and mixing up potions?"

"I hated Ruthersfield," Poppy would snap with such force that Cat always let the conversation drop.

One day, unable to help herself, Cat climbed onto a smooth chestnut broomstick leaning against the side of the bakery. The teacher it belonged to came every week to buy a loaf of her mother's walnut bread. She didn't look much older than some of the year-twelve girls, with her bouncy brown curls and smooth skin, but instead of a uniform she dressed in the long purple gown the teachers wore.

"Fly," Cat ordered the broomstick, jumping off the ground. She imagined how it would feel, soaring through the air, and Cat jumped again and again, but each time she landed with a thud.

"Do you think I might have my broomstick back, please?" the woman said, coming out of the shop, a bag of warm bread in her arms.

"Gosh, I'm so sorry," Cat apologized, blushing with embarrassment as she handed the broomstick over. "I was very careful with it. I just wish I could fly."

"It is fun," the woman admitted, holding out her hand. "I'm Clara Bell, by the way. I teach magical history at Ruthersfield. And your mother makes the best bread in Potts Bottom. Actually she makes the best bread I've ever had."

"Yes, she's an excellent baker," Cat agreed with a sigh. "But baking is so boring. I want to be a witch, just like you. My mum got the gift, but she doesn't use it anymore, and my great-great-grandmother Mabel was an amazing witch. She invented all kinds of brilliant things."

"Well, don't give up yet," Clara Bell said, tucking

the bread into her satchel. "I was ten when I showed my first sign of magic. A Late Bloomer," she added with a smile.

"What happened?" Cat said eagerly, bouncing up and down. "How did it feel?"

"I was taking a shower, and I remember thinking what a boring color water was, and all of a sudden it started to run this lovely shade of lavender." Clara Bell laughed at the memory. "I felt all tingly inside, as if my magic was fizzing."

"Oh, I wish that would happen to me."

But by the time Cat turned eleven, it was clear she had not inherited her mother's magical gene, although every time she blew out her birthday candles or saw a shooting star, that was the wish Cat made.

"Never mind, Cat, love," her father said, giving her one of his big bear hugs. "When you're a little bit older you can come with me on some of my research trips. Being a botanist may not be magical, but it's full of excitement. I'd never have discovered that new species of moss if I hadn't got lost on a mountain in Tanzania."

"Thanks, Dad," Cat replied, unable to quite give up on her dream.

Her mother was relieved. Cat knew that. Poppy couldn't hide her feelings toward magic, although she hated seeing her daughter so sad. "We'll find you a passion you can do," Poppy suggested, buying Cat ice skates, a paint set, and a tennis racket. She signed her daughter up for gymnastics classes, horseback riding, and rock climbing. But although Cat had fun and enjoyed trying new things, nothing could take away her desire to be a witch. The one thing in the world she couldn't have.

Chapter Two

....

The Fear of Madeline Reynolds

CAT BURST THROUGH THE DOOR OF THE BAKERY, bringing with her a swirl of crisp November air. "We're doing a project at school, Mamma," she called out. "We have to dress up as the person from history we most admire and write a biography on them."

"Oh, what fun!" Poppy said, handing Maxine Gibbons a bag of warm almond cakes. Maxine had lived next door to Poppy's parents in their little brick house on Pudding Lane for almost fifty years, and knew everything there was to know about the family. In fact, Maxine Gibbons knew everything there was to know about most people in Potts Bottom.

"Who are you going to choose?" Maxine asked, tucking the cakes in her basket. Her dark eyes gleamed with interest, and the whiskers on her chin quivered through their dusting of powder. Cat saw her mother glance at the door and knew she wanted Maxine to leave, but Maxine obviously had no intention of budging. She looked straight at Cat and gave a sly smile. At least it looked sly to Cat. "I'll never forget when your mother was at Ruthersfield, Cat; she had to do a biography project too. Remember that, Poppy?"

Poppy slammed the till shut and glared at Maxine. "I'm surprised you do. That was a long time ago."

"Oh, I remember it like it was yesterday," Maxine said, giving a little shiver. "You did yours on Madeline Reynolds, didn't you? The most dangerous witch in the world. I get chills just thinking about her."

"Mamma, is that true?" Cat said in alarm. "You actually chose Madeline Reynolds?"

"Maxine!" Poppy fumed. "Was that really necessary? Or do you just enjoy frightening Cat by bringing up Madeline Reynolds? Because this wouldn't be the first time, would it?"

"All I said—" Maxine began, but Poppy cut her off.

"I know what you said. And have you forgotten that it was you who scared Cat to tears when she was only four years old? Four!" Poppy shouted. "Right here in the bakery. She hadn't even heard of Madeline Reynolds, but you had to go and tell her in vivid Maxine detail all the awful things she'd done. How she'd washed away half of Italy with one of her spells." Cat's mother rarely lost her temper, but the way she swished her braid over her shoulder and grabbed a croissant made Cat wonder if she was about to throw it at Maxine. "Do you know I still have to check under Cat's bed sometimes, just to make sure Madeline Reynolds isn't hiding there? Which by the way is impossible," Poppy added, "because Madeline Reynolds is locked up in Scrubs Prison and is never ever getting out." She put her hands on the counter, crushing the croissant, and took a couple of deep breaths. "Honestly, Maxine, I have never understood why you felt the need to tell Cat about her in the first place."

Cat noticed the look Maxine gave her mother, as if they both shared a secret and weren't saying. "Well, I thought Cat should know," Maxine said with a huff. "Having such a big interest in magic the way she always has."

"You gave her nightmares for years," Poppy shouted, as Marie Claire came hobbling out of the kitchen. "So why you'd go and mention her again is beyond me."

"Is everything all right?" Marie Claire said. She slipped an arm around Cat's waist. "What is going on?"

"Maxine was just leaving, weren't you?" Poppy snapped, marching over to the door and opening it.

"Well, really!" Maxine said, and clutching her basket against her, she scurried out of the bakery.

Cat gave a nervous laugh. "I thought you were going to throw that croissant at her head, Mamma! You looked so mad."

"Honestly, Maxine drives me nuts," Poppy said, managing a smile at Cat. "Always stirring the pot. Let's not waste another breath on that woman."

"And I haven't had nightmares about Madeline Reynolds for years," Cat pointed out. "I just like you to check under my bed sometimes because it's part of our old routine."

Marie Claire cleared her throat. "So how was school today?" she asked in her softly faded French accent, tactfully changing the subject. She had lived at the bakery with Cat and her parents for as long as Cat could remember, helping her mother with all the cooking and keeping them company when Cat's father, Tristram, was off having one of his adventures.

"I have to dress up as my favorite person in history and write a paper about her," Cat said.

"And who will you choose?" Poppy asked, straightening a row of cupcakes.

Cat wanted to say Mabel Ratcliff, her great-great-grandmother who had invented a way to harvest star power and had helped design one of the first rocket broomsticks to fly to the moon. But what she was most well-known for was her amazing quick-growing hair potion that came in a wonderful array of colors. Curly autumn leaf, which was a lovely deep red, and burnt caramel, which looked all glossy and smooth and made you want to lick it. Because of Mabel Ratcliff's hair invention, baldness was a thing of the past, and even though Cat hadn't inherited the family magic gene, she was still unbelievably proud of her great-great-grandmother. "I'm not sure yet," Cat began, knowing that if she mentioned Mabel Ratcliff, her mother's face would get that tight, stressed look, the way it always did whenever Cat brought up anything to do with witchcraft. And she hated upsetting her mother. They could talk about everything else in the whole world, except Cat's love of magic.

"Maybe Antonia Bigglesmith?" Cat said, thinking her idea out loud. "She was the first woman to fly an airplane all the way across the Indian Ocean, all by herself." The shop bell tinkled and a group of Ruthersfield girls walked into the bakery. Cat couldn't help staring at their smart purple uniforms with the thin gold trim around the edges. "Antonia Bigglesmith was an adventurer just like Dad," Cat continued quietly.

"Well, Tristram would approve of that!" Poppy said. "No one loves adventure more than he does."

Cat swallowed the ache in her throat. She missed her father so much when he was traveling. His research as a botanist took him all over the world. At this very moment he was off exploring the mountains of Zangezur, looking for a rare type of plant that one of the local tribes claimed had extraordinary healing properties.

"You know my dad used to have an old pilot's cap," Poppy said. "It was one his father wore in the war. You should ask Grandpa if he still has it," she suggested. "That would be perfect for your costume."

"Oh, Mum, that's a great idea! Can I go now?" Cat said, wanting to take a look at the broomsticks parked out front, before their owners flew off.

"Just be back in time for dinner," Poppy called after her as Cat hurried out of the shop. "The Parkers are coming."

Propped up against the wall of the bakery were four brooms. Three were made of a light, honey-colored wood, and one was a dark cherry. Cat ran her hands up and down the cherry one, feeling the smoothness of the grain beneath her fingers. She closed her eyes, imagining what it must be like to swoop across the sky.

"Excuse me, that's mine," one of the Ruthersfield

girls said, grabbing her broom from Cat. "Please don't touch it."

"I'm sorry," Cat murmured, stepping back. "It's just so beautiful."

The girl didn't answer. She climbed on and turned her head away, waiting for her friends to mount. Then, with a chorus of giggling, the four girls swooped into the air, following the path alongside the canal. Cat stared after them, watching the girls shrink to the size of purple birds. It was only then that she wondered why her mother had picked Madeline Reynolds for a biography project. Why not Mabel Ratcliff or some other wonderful witch? Madeline Reynolds was the worst storm brewer in history. What possible appeal could she have had for her mother? Cat wished Maxine Gibbons hadn't mentioned it.

Chapter Three

....

An Exciting Discovery

CAT LOVED TO VISIT HER GRANDPARENTS IN THEIR little brick house on Pudding Lane. She set off in the same direction as the broomstick riders. The Ribbald Valley, where Potts Bottom nestled, was tinged with autumn colors, and in the distance, Cat could see the swell of fields and hills, still speckled with purple heather. As she walked, she threw a stone across the canal, trying to hit the woods on the other side. At one time, back in the last century, the canal had been a bustling waterway, but now the most traffic it ever got was the odd pleasure barge or a family of ducks floating down.

Her path veered off to the right, and Cat started to run, heading up the well-worn track into town. She wound her way through the narrow streets. A lot of the homes in Potts Bottom had been built close together, so you could often see neighbors chatting over fences and washing flapping on clotheslines. Cat always took the same route, balancing on top of garden walls with the speed and agility of a cat. She even looked like one, with her sleek marmalade-colored hair and green eyes. Occasionally Cat managed to reach number 10 Pudding Lane without once touching the pavement. There was one big leap between Mrs. Miller's house and Maxine's where Cat often fell, but she loved the challenge of trying, even if she did sometimes end up with scraped knees. This afternoon, though, Cat leaped across perfectly, imagining she was flying on a broomstick.

"Catkins!" Granny Edith cried, opening the door. "What a lovely surprise!" She spread her arms wide, and Cat flew into them.

"I'm doing a project on Antonia Bigglesmith, Granny, and I need a costume. Mamma thought Grandpa might still have an old pilot's cap of his dad's, which would be perfect."

"Oh, I don't know," Granny Edith said, shepherding

Cat into the kitchen. "Roger, it's Catkins," she called out, switching off the television.

Cat smiled at her grandfather, who was sitting at the table with a cup of tea. She kissed the top of his silvery hair, thick and soft as a lion's mane thanks to Granny Mabel's hair potion.

"How's my favorite granddaughter?" Roger Pendle said, getting to his feet. He always greeted Cat that way, which she found rather funny because she was their only granddaughter. "Did you bring me some of your mum's coconut cupcakes?"

"Now, don't go pestering Cat for cupcakes, Roger. It's not like you need any."

"Sorry, Grandpa, I forgot," Cat said, noticing that her grandfather's cardigan did seem to be having difficulty stretching across his middle.

"Cat's here on a mission," Edith Pendle said. "She wants that old pilot's hat of your dad's. You know the one, with the furry flaps."

"Oh, I've no idea where that is." Roger Pendle shook his head. "You did that big clean-out a few years ago, Edith."

"Well, I wouldn't have thrown the cap away. It's probably in the attic somewhere, if you felt like having a look, Cat."

"Bit of a mess up there," Roger Pendle said. "And you better watch out for spiders, Catkins!"

"That's not funny, Grandpa!" Cat said, trying hard not to smile. She'd always had a powerful fear of spiders, and one Christmas dinner a few years ago, Grandpa Roger had got a trick plastic one in his Christmas cracker. Cat still got embarrassed, thinking about how loud she had screamed when she saw it, knocking her bowl of pudding onto the floor. Even though most of the spiders she came across were small, harmless things, it still made her palms sweat and her skin tingle whenever she saw one scuttling around on its hairy legs. "Will you come up with me, Gran?" Cat said. "Show me where to look?"

"I'm not sure I know, dear. Just have a poke about. It'll be in one of the boxes."

Granny Edith led Cat upstairs. At the top of the landing was a narrow door with an old-fashioned key in the lock.

"I can never get this thing to turn," Granny Edith said, jiggling the key about. "It always sticks for me." She gave a frustrated huff. "You have a go, Cat."

Cat grasped the large iron key. She wiggled it back and forth a few times, and finally managed to twist the key around. Pressing the handle down, Cat tugged the door, which opened with a stiff creak.

"Well done, Kitty Cat." Granny Edith reached inside and flipped on the light switch. "Now, be careful going up."

The stairs to the attic were narrow and steep. Cat pressed against the walls as she climbed. A gritty layer of dirt covered each tread, and she guessed that her grandparents hadn't been up here in quite some time.

"If you can't find the cap, just give me a shout," Granny Edith called up.

"Don't worry, Gran, I'll be fine," Cat replied, stepping into the attic. A powerful tang of mothballs greeted her. The air was so thick with dust Cat could almost taste it. Looking around, she saw a cradle and high chair that must have been used by her mother when she was a baby, an old sewing machine, a stack of checkered suitcases, and piles of cardboard boxes. Wispy cobwebs dangled from the beams, but they were ancient and tattered and spiders hadn't lived there in a long time. This felt like Christmas, Cat decided, picking her way across the floor. Who knew what treasures might be hidden in these boxes? Although Cat found out pretty quickly the answer to that was not many. Being careful to keep an eye out for spiders, she unearthed some gardening tools, a set of brown spotted china, some old hairbrushes, and three boxes of *Train Spotter* magazine. There were a couple of bulging plastic bags slumped in a corner. Cat rooted through them, pulling out a sparkly beaded dress that smelled of Granny Edith's face powder and a green velvet jacket full of moth holes, but no pilot's cap.

Giving a sigh of disappointment, Cat glanced around the attic. Where would Granny Edith have put the cap? she wondered. On the far north side, Cat noticed a small window built into one of the eaves. It was covered in grime, so there was little light coming through, but enough for Cat to see a crawl space underneath. Being careful not to tread on any loose boards, she made her way across to it. Getting down on her knees, Cat peered into the crawl space. Tucked right at the back so they were difficult to see were two cardboard boxes. Coughing from the dust, Cat tugged them out, one at a time. This looked like the sort of place you would keep something important. And sure enough, when she opened the first box, underneath a mound of loose papers and maps, Cat pulled out an old aviation cap. The leather was stiff and cracked with age, and moths had nibbled the fur around the edges, but it would be perfect for her costume. There was even a pair of goggles to go over the cap, and with the maps as accessories she would look just like Antonia Bigglesmith!

This was fantastic, and maybe, if she were lucky,

Cat thought, she would find a vintage flying jacket in the next box. Tugging open the flaps, Cat peered inside. There were some neatly folded clothes on top, and underneath them a pile of books. Not quite understanding what she had discovered, Cat put the clothes aside and lifted out the books one at a time. *"Simple Spells,"* she whispered, blowing off the dust and reading the title. Cat paused and looked again to make sure she hadn't been mistaken. A spell book! A real spell book! She could feel her heart pounding in her chest as she pulled out *The Fine Art of Wand Technique, Practical Magic, The Compendium of Witchcraft Cookery,* and with a muffled shriek of delight, a heavy, thick volume called *Advanced Magic.*

Where had all of these books come from? Cat puzzled. It was only when she took out a stack of composition notebooks and journals that she realized what she had found. These were her mother's things from Ruthersfield. The books she had used to study magic. On the front of them all, in rather messy handwriting, was her mother's name and the name of the class. There were notebooks for spell chanting, potions class, palm reading . . . and Cat stared at each one in amazement. "Oh, my goodness," she whispered. "Flipping fish cakes!" Cat's mouth had gone dry and she was breathing loud and fast.

She picked up a purple cardboard folder with "Miss Jenkins's History Class — Biography Project" written across the top. Inside were some photocopies of old newspaper articles clipped together, and underneath them on lined white paper was her mother's essay, titled "The Life and Times of Madeline Reynolds, by Poppy Pendle." A large red A was scrawled in the margin, which showed what a good student her mother had been. And she had clearly done her research. Unclipping the articles, Cat shuffled through them. The headlines jumped out at her in bold black print.

SHOCK AND HORROR AS WITCH PRODIGY BREWS UP HISTORIC STORM.

HUNDREDS LOSE THEIR LIVES WHEN MADELINE REYNOLDS WASHES AWAY HALF OF ITALY.

CROWDS CHEER AS WORLD'S MOST EVIL WITCH IS LOCKED UP IN SCRUBS.

WHAT MADE A RUTHERSFIELD ALUMNA GO OVER TO THE DARK SIDE?

Cat shoved the clippings back inside the folder and slammed it shut. This was too disturbing for her to read any more. She pushed the folder under the crawl space as far back as it would go, needing to get it out of her sight. Surely her mother must have been assigned Madeline Reynolds for this project, because no one in her right mind would choose to study such an evil witch, would she? Cat had to admit that she was definitely not over her childhood fear, and under normal circumstances she would have bolted out of the attic fast. But these were not normal circumstances, and she had no intention of leaving now. Who knew what else might be hidden in the box? Taking some deep, calming breaths, Cat reminded herself that Madeline Reynolds was safely locked away in Scrubs Prison. And she, Cat Campbell, had just made the discovery of a lifetime.

Reaching for the clothes, Cat shook out a skirt, sweater, and jacket. They were a deep royal purple, although the sweater had faded with time. But there was no mistaking the logo on the jacket pocket, a cauldron with two crossed broomsticks and the words "Ruthersfield Academy" embroidered in cursive script underneath. Cat held the uniform up to her face, inhaling magic and dreams and all the things she wanted so badly. A faint smell of baking clung to it, which didn't surprise Cat one bit. She dug her hand into one of the jacket pockets and pulled out some fossilized crumbs. What if she put it on? Cat thought, glancing around the attic. No one would know. It couldn't do any harm. Quickly and with shaking fingers, Cat slipped on the Ruthersfield uniform. The clothes fit her perfectly, and smoothing down the skirt, she twirled around, wishing there was a mirror in the attic so she could see her reflection. "Hello, I'm a witch. I go to Ruthersfield," Cat whispered, wishing with all her heart that this was true.

Kneeling beside the box again, she felt around inside to see what else was there. "A mini practice cauldron!" Cat squealed, lifting out a small brass pot with a handle. It had drips down the side from a long ago spell, and Cat wondered what her mother had made. She balanced the cauldron on top of the books, admiring it for a moment, before running her hands around the bottom of the box. Stuck to the cardboard, right along the edge so Cat almost missed it, was a long, thick object that felt a bit like a giant pencil. Peeling it free with her fingernails, Cat held it up and shrieked, clamping a hand over her mouth because she didn't want her grandparents coming up. It wasn't a giant pencil at all. It was a magic wand! Her mother's old magic wand, Cat guessed, covered in bits of lint and fluff and something that still felt sticky. Knowing her mother, she had probably used it to stir cake batter.

"A real wand!" Cat whispered, waving it about. "A real magic wand." Her heart was racing as she pointed it across the attic. "Alicadaze," Cat said, spinning around and pointing it at the window. "Abercazoo, Zapadido." Nothing happened, of course. She tapped the wand against her leg and waved it at the high chair. "Fluttertijack, Mollyticock," Cat cried out, longing to say magic words and do magic things. A yearning so strong and deep swept over Cat that she leaned against the window, pressing her face to the dusty glass. This was all she had ever wanted, to be a real witch and go to Ruthersfield Academy. But that was never going to happen. Cat almost wished she hadn't found these things. None of this was real. It was dress up, pretend, and she slid to the floor in dejection. She was no more a witch than she was Antonia Bigglesmith.

For a few minutes Cat sat slumped against the wall, staring at the stack of magic books. She let out a deep sigh, knowing she should take off the uniform and go downstairs. Her grandparents would be wondering what had happened to her. It was as Cat started to get up that she felt a gentle tickling on her leg. With her free hand Cat scratched at her shin, and something scuttled onto her fingers. She looked down and screamed, waving her arm about in a frenzy. A huge hairy spider, the kind with a fat body and thick legs, was crawling across her hand. Feeling like she was about to vomit, Cat gave a violent shake and the spider dropped into her lap. Panic coursed through her and she screamed again, flicking the spider onto the floor with the wand. A strange tingling sensation fizzed along Cat's spine, and the spider immediately puffed up to the size of a golf ball, turning bright neon green. Scrambling to her feet, Cat gave a muffled howl as the spider turned violet, then orange, then yellow. She backed away, still watching as it began to glow indigo blue, pulsing between all the colors of the rainbow like a crazy disco ball. This wasn't normal. Cat knew that. Spiders did not behave like this, even the most deadly kind. Hardly daring to believe what was happening, Cat clambered onto the high chair and pointed her wand at the creature again. She felt the same delicious, tingly feeling, which was just as Clara Bell had described, and the spider began bouncing around the room.

"Are you all right, Catkins?" her grandmother called up. "Grandpa thought he heard you scream."

"I'm f-fine, Gran," Cat panted, watching the spider bounce about like a rubber ball, hitting the walls and ceiling and continuously changing colors. "Never been better!" she called down, clamping her lips together to stop herself from screaming out, "I'm magic! I've got the gift! I'm a Late Bloomer like Clara Bell." It was all Cat could do not to charge around the attic doing cartwheels. This was the moment she'd been waiting for her whole life. And now that it was here, she wanted to shout it all over Potts Bottom.

The spider gave a particularly high bounce and landed smack in the middle of a large, sticky web that hung from a corner of the attic. There was a strong smell of licorice, a sweet, dark, treacly scent that must have been what magic smelled like. Cat was relieved to see that the spider appeared to be trapped. It had stopped moving and changing color, staying a lovely shade of magenta that reminded Cat of an enormous jewel caught in the web.

"Did you find the cap?" Edith shouted up as Cat took off the uniform, trembling all over with excitement. Her hands shook as she put the clothes back in the box, squashing them on top of the books and mini cauldron.

"I did. I found a lot of great things I can use," Cat yelled, stuffing the pilot's cap in too. The wand Cat kissed and slipped into her pocket, pulling her sweater down so you couldn't see the tip. It was far too precious to let go of. She gave a soft laugh and did a little dance. "I've got the gene," Cat whispered, picking up the box. "I've really got the gene."

She couldn't tell anyone yet though, not even her grandparents, not until she had figured out how to tell her mother first. And that wasn't going to be easy, especially when Cat told her mother that she wanted to apply to Ruthersfield Academy.

Chapter Four

Out of Control

GRANDPA ROGER HAD DRIVEN CAT AS FAR AS THE
narrow canal path would allow him, so she
wouldn't have to walk the whole way home lugging the
box of stuff. Luckily, after showing her grandparents
the pilot's cap, Granny Edith had waved her hands at
Cat and said, "Take that dusty box out of my kitchen,
Cat. Whatever's inside, you're welcome to it."

Now, as Cat walked along the gravel path that led to
the bakery, she felt as if she was hugging an enormous
box of secrets. Secrets so special and amazing that she
didn't care how heavy the box was or how much her

arms ached; she had never been happier in her life. The air was crisp and fresh, laced with the tang of wood smoke, and a harvest moon hung low in the sky, reflecting its light off the canal.

"I've got the gift!" Cat whispered, needing to say the words out loud because she still couldn't really believe it.

There was a sweet, spicy scent wafting from the bakery, and Cat knew that her mother was making gingerbread. The shop door was closed, so Cat staggered around to the back, sending the chickens scattering. They lived in a little coop that Cat's dad had built, but most of the time the chickens roamed freely around the yard, gobbling up stale cake and bread crumbs that Poppy and Marie Claire threw out for them. Light streamed through the kitchen window, and Cat could see her mother pulling a pan of gingerbread out of the oven. Auntie Charlie and Uncle Tom were sitting by the fire with Marie Claire, and Peter's lanky frame was sprawled across the table, sketching something out on a piece of paper. His glasses had slipped down his nose and he appeared to be talking to himself, which was not uncommon for Peter. Cat had forgotten that the Parkers were coming for supper. Not that she minded. Even though Auntie Charlie and Uncle Tom weren't her real aunt and uncle, Cat adored them as if they were family. Auntie Charlie and her mother had been best friends since they were girls, and Auntie Charlie still came over most days. When Peter and Cat were little, they had spent hours and hours playing on the bakery floor together, making up games and squabbling over the crayons and blocks. Being only children, they felt more like brother and sister than friends. Cat was very fond of Peter, but like all siblings, they were excellent at annoying each other too. And since Peter had joined the science club and spent most of his time making weird inventions these days, the annoying part of him was definitely getting bigger!

Cat tapped on the back door with her shoe, unable to use her hands. She smiled through the glass pane as her mother rushed over to open it. "Gracious, Cat! What on earth did you find?"

"A pilot's cap and a few other things" Cat said, lurching into the kitchen. "Hi, Auntie Charlie. Hi, Uncle Tom."

"Hey, that looks heavy. Where do you want it?" Uncle Tom said, leaping to his feet. He always looked like a giant in the bakery because, at six and a half feet tall, his head nearly touched the ceiling. Cat guessed he had come straight from work, since he still wore his uniform. Uncle Tom was the Potts Bottom chief of police.

"I'll just take this up to my room. Thanks, Uncle Tom," Cat said, resting her chin on the box to make sure the flaps were down. "I'll be right back," she added, shuffling across the kitchen. Cat caught Peter watching her, and when he noticed she was looking, he raised his bushy eyebrows and grinned. It was as if he knew she was carrying a great big secret, and Cat turned her head away, pointedly ignoring him.

She hurried as fast as a person can hurry carrying a heavy box of magic books and a mini brass cauldron upstairs to her room. There were three little bedrooms on the second floor of the cottage, and the bakery, kitchen, and a small living room down below. As Cat shoved the box under her bed, a cloud of dust floated up, and she darted over to open her window; otherwise she'd be coughing all night. Then, wiping her hands on her skirt, Cat raced back to the kitchen.

Her mother was just putting a roast chicken down in the middle of the table. She clapped her hands. "Clear your stuff off, please, Peter. And, Cat, knives and forks."

"What are you doing?" Cat asked, glancing at the piece of paper in front of Peter. It looked just the way his bits of paper always looked, filled with squiggles and numbers and odd little shapes.

"I'm figuring out how to make an earthquake

detector," Peter said, brushing back a clump of black curls from his face. They sprung from his head in a wild, frizzy mass that always made Cat want to reach for the scissors.

"Well, you never know when that will come in handy," Cat said. "Considering there's never been a single earthquake in Potts Bottom as far as I know!"

"It's going to pick up small vibrations in the earth," Peter said, helping Cat put knives and forks around the table. "And just because we've never had an earthquake, Cat, doesn't mean we won't get one."

"We might get hit by an asteroid, too!" Uncle Tom joked gently, and Cat couldn't help laughing, because for weeks and weeks Peter had convinced most of the kids at school that an enormous asteroid was en route to hit the earth. He had worked out the exact time and day it would happen, judging from the speed and direction the asteroid was traveling, and a great many other facts that no one else could understand. So at eight thirty a.m. on Tuesday, September 25, most of the kids from Potts Bottom Elementary had refused to go to school and taken shelter in their cellars. A number of kindergartners had apparently been in hysterics, and when the asteroid didn't hit, hordes of angry parents had turned up at the Parkers' house demanding to know what Peter was playing at, scaring their children half to death.

"I wasn't off by much in my asteroid calculations," Peter replied calmly. "It was entirely possible."

"Well, I think your earthquake sensor sounds very interesting," Marie Claire said, hobbling over to the stove. She picked up a pan of potatoes.

"Marie Claire, I'll do that," Cat offered, rushing over to help. "You look like your ankle is hurting."

"It's a little achy today, but nothing that your mother's dinner won't put right."

The meal was delicious, although Cat couldn't eat a thing. She was far too excited, and every few seconds she would pat her pocket, unable to resist the temptation to feel the magic wand.

"Cat, are you looking for something?" Poppy finally asked. "You seem very distracted."

"No, just thinking about my Antonia Bigglesmith project. And I had two Twirlie bars at Gran's house," Cat admitted. "So I'm not really hungry." This was true, but it certainly didn't account for her loss of appetite.

"Oh, Cat, how can you eat those things?" Poppy sighed. "They're full of additives and preservatives."

"And taste heavenly," Cat pointed out, smiling at her mother. She loved the soft vanilla-flavored cake and sweet cream filling of a Twirlie bar. So what if they had a shelf life of a hundred years? They were

Cat's favorite treat in the entire world. She would take a Twirlie bar over a homemade cupcake any day of the week.

As the dinner wore on, Cat found it harder and harder not to say anything. She kept squirming about on her chair and had to press her lips together to stop her news from bubbling out. She would explode if she didn't tell someone.

"Cat, have you got fleas?" Peter asked, leaning forward and claiming the last roast potato. "Because you're starting to make me feel itchy."

"I have to show you something," Cat burst out. "This old pilot's cap that belonged to my great-granddad. It's going to be part of my costume."

"Really?" Peter looked surprised.

"I just told you I was going as Antonia Bigglesmith."

"No, I don't mean 'really' about that. I mean, really, you want to show me?"

"Go on," Poppy said. "We'll do the dishes and call you down when it's time for dessert. It's nice to see you two working on your projects together. Who are you going as, Peter?"

"Herbert Onsteen!" Peter said, getting up from the table. "Greatest inventor who ever lived."

"You don't need a costume then, do you?" Cat said, grinning. "You're tall, you've got the mad scientist hair! Little bits of paper sticking out of your pockets."

"This better be quick," Peter muttered, following Cat out of the kitchen. "Because I'm not missing your mum's gingerbread."

"Wait till you see what I'm going to show you," Cat said, charging up the stairs.

"Well, I know it's not a pilot's cap," Peter replied, lolloping after her.

Cat pulled him into her bedroom and shut the door. "Peter, the most amazing thing happened this afternoon. You are not going to believe it!"

"Why are you telling me then?"

"I can't tell my mum, or my friends. Not that you're not a friend," Cat added hastily. "But you know what I mean."

"Do I?" Peter sat down on Cat's bed.

"Yes, of course you do. You're a good secret keeper."

"Ahhh, so that's it. You have to tell someone, and you know I won't blab to Auntie Poppy. Oh, look at this!" Peter said, picking up a strange contraption from the floor. Rolls of cardboard tubes had been fastened together at right angles with duct tape. "You still have the periscope I made you in year one—for checking under your bed to make sure Madeline Reynolds wasn't hiding there, remember? Look." Peter demonstrated, peering through one end and putting the other end under the bed. "Wow, I did a great job with the mirrors," he added, admiring his handiwork.

"Put it down," Cat said, looking slightly embarrassed. "That was a long time ago. I never use it anymore."

"Which is why it still lives by your bed, right?"

"Just put that down and listen, will you," Cat said impatiently, pulling the wand out of her pocket.

"What on earth . . ." Peter began, staring at the wand.

"I know!" Cat jumped up and down. "It's real, Peter. I'm magic!!!"

"Wait, that's a real wand?" Peter held out his hand. "Can I look at it?" He leaned forward and Cat handed him the wand.

"Did you hear me?" She twirled around. "I'm magic! I've got the gift! I'm a Late Bloomer, Peter."

"Where on earth did you find this?" Peter said, examining the wand.

"In my gran and grandpa's attic, along with all my mum's old magic books." Cat tugged the box out from under the bed and held up *Simple Spells*. "See!"

"Cat, I don't mean to burst your bubble here, but just because you've found your mum's old wand, doesn't mean you're magic."

"I made a spider change color, Peter. Lots of colors.

And it grew and bounced around the attic, and—"

"Cat," Peter interrupted, handing her back the wand. "You have an extremely vivid imagination. Remember that time you thought you made a stick roll, but it was really the wind? Or the time you made a rain spell, and when it rained two days later, you thought that was because of you?"

"This was different, Peter. I felt all tingly and magical!" Cat shivered at the memory. "It was the most delicious sensation." She opened *Simple Spells*, and started to flip through it. "Look, I'll show you. I'll do a spell."

"Well, make it quick, because I'm ready for my gingerbread."

"I should start with something easy, don't you think? How about this? A simple room tidying spell?" Cat glanced around her bedroom. Her jacket and scarf and gloves were still lying in a heap where she had taken them off, and yesterday's clothes were scattered across the floor.

"Go on then," Peter said, yawning.

"Can you open my cupboard so the clothes can hang themselves up?"

With a loud sigh, Peter walked over to Cat's cupboard and tugged it open. He folded his arms and rolled his eyes.

"I know you don't believe me, Peter, but you will! I'm so excited, I can hardly stand it." Cat glanced at the page, then, waving her wand around the room, she cried out, "Tiddlylischus!"

Nothing happened, and Peter gave a crooked smile. "I think you're holding your wand upside down, Cat."

"I am? Oh yes, you're right, Peter. The tip should go the other way, shouldn't it?" Cat flipped the wand around and tried again. "Tiddlylischus!" she shouted.

Still nothing happened, and Peter chuckled. "Should I be using my imagination here?"

Cat glared at him. "I am not making this up."

Shaking his head, Peter strolled across the room and glanced down at the page. "Okay, Cat, seriously! That says 'Tidylischus,' not 'Tiddlylischus'! You've got to be able to say the words right!"

Ignoring Peter's comment, Cat tried again. "Tidylischus!" she said, making a sweeping motion with the wand. Immediately all the clothes on the floor floated into the air, and Cat danced around in delight. "It's working, Peter, it's working." She watched them tumble and swirl as if they were in a dryer, but instead of hanging themselves up in the cupboard like the spell said they would, the clothes started moving faster. "Oh dear, I don't think I've got it quite right," Cat said, as her red wool sweater grabbed Peter by the arms, tugging him across the room.

"Hey, get off me," Peter cried, as the sweater spun him around like a dance partner.

Cat's scarf was speeding in circles, and every time it flew by Cat, it whipped her in the face. Not knowing quite what to do, she gave a panicky laugh. "Into the cupboard!" Cat ordered a pair of black socks that were dipping and diving at them like bats. Her jeans waved their legs about, racing away from Cat every time she tried to grab one. "Peter, help me," she panted. "I can't control them."

"No kidding," Peter gasped, wrestling with the sweater. "Will you go away?"

Cat managed to grab on to her puffy winter jacket as it spun by. She dragged it across the room and, with a great deal of pushing and shoving, got it into the cupboard and slammed the door shut behind it. "Oh, no, the window," Cat groaned, turning to see her jeans squeezing through the opening. At least they were her old ones with the holes in the knees. Her socks and gloves sped out after them, quickly followed by Cat's scarf and T-shirt. Her sweater had pinned Peter to the floor, and Cat yanked at the neck, trying to pull it off him. "I never liked wearing you," Cat said, pulling as hard as she could. "You were always too scratchy!"

Noticing the other clothes leave, the sweater abruptly let go of Peter and dashed off after them, pushing Cat out of the way as if it didn't want to get left behind. She raced to the window to try to grab an arm, but it was too late. The sweater waved a sleeve at her, and by the light of the moon Cat watched it dance off along the canal.

"Wow!" Peter said, moving to stand beside her. His face was flushed red.

"So you believe me now?" Cat giggled nervously as she shut the window.

"You're going to have to tell your mum."

"But I'm scared, Peter. You know how she feels about magic. What if she doesn't let me apply to Ruthersfield?"

"You've got to tell her, Cat. That is not normal magic."

"Well, I haven't had any practice. That's why I need to go to the academy. So they can teach me how to do spells."

"Crikey!" Peter shook his head. "Crikey," he said again. "I'm not sure I could eat any gingerbread after that. I've completely lost my appetite."

"I wish my dad were here," Cat sighed. "He would understand how exciting this is. He'd help me tell my mum."

"When's he coming back?" Peter asked.

Cat gave a small shrug. "I don't know, Peter. I hope soon. He's searching for a rare species of plant and he won't come back until he finds it. That's how my dad is. He doesn't give up easily." It was always hard when her father went away on one of his trips, and although Cat tried not to worry, it was impossible to stop the scared feelings from building up inside her.

Chapter Five

· ·

Flipping Fish Cakes!

C AT WAS RELIEVED WHEN THE PARKERS FINALLY LEFT
that evening. She needed to be alone, to think
about what had just happened. Peter had made her
promise to tell her mother, and Cat wanted to—she
really did—just not tonight. She couldn't face the conversation she knew they would have when her mother
found out Cat was a Late Bloomer. *I'll tell her tomorrow,*
Cat promised herself, *right after school.* That way she
could figure out exactly what to say. Besides, she still
had her homework to do, which, in all the excitement
of the afternoon, Cat had completely forgotten about.

Tristram Campbell had built Cat a little desk in the

corner of her room. It was the perfect place to do her homework; her books always got covered in flour whenever she sat at the kitchen table. But Cat found it impossible to concentrate on Antonia Bigglesmith with her jacket moving about in the cupboard. Every time it gave a muffled thud, a nervous thrill shot through her and Cat glanced at the door, anxious that her mother might hear. It was slightly unnerving, having an uncontrollable coat in her cupboard. She obviously needed more practice with her spells, but at least some magic had happened.

Cat impulsively reached for the airplane note cards Marie Claire had given her last Christmas, opening up one with a vintage stunt plane on the front. Cat wrote in purple ink:

Dear Dad,

I hope you are well. I miss you sooooooo much. Guess what? You are not going to believe this, but (and you will know how happy I am!) I've inherited the magic gene. I'm a Late Bloomer. I've got the gift!!!!!!!!!!!!!!!!! There's going to be another witch in the family. Are you surprised? I wish you were here to help me tell Mum because I want to try out for Rutherfield. I'm so excited. When are you coming home?

Love, Cat
xoxoxox

Slipping the card into an envelope, Cat gave a satisfied sigh. She would post the letter tomorrow. It would take ages to get to Zangezur—Cat knew that—but she had a strong feeling that when her father read it, he would understand how important this was and come right home.

Cat yawned and tapped her pen against her teeth. Her eyes felt heavy and tired even though her mind was still racing. The magic books seemed to be calling out to her. "Just a little peek," they were saying. "One little peek and then you can go back to your homework." Bending over her journal, Cat scribbled, "Antonia Bigglesmith was born in 1927 in Clacton-by-the-Sea." She yawned again and pushed back her chair. One little peek wouldn't hurt, surely? She'd just read through a couple of spells and then finish drafting her essay on Antonia Bigglesmith.

Kneeling on the floor, Cat opened *Practical Magic*. Some of the pages were stuck together, which made Cat smile, because when she put her tongue against the paper she could taste something sweet. Obviously her mother used to do her homework while she baked! Very carefully Cat peeled the pages apart, taking in the dusty book smell mingled with the faint fizz of old magic that tickled her nostrils and made her want to sneeze.

"Moving a simple object," Cat read. That looked like a fun spell. All you did was wave your wand at something and say . . . Cat peered at the word and mouthed it slowly. "Aloftdisimo." She said it over and over again, letting the strange sounds roll off her tongue. "Aloftdisimo, Aloftdisimo, Aloftdisimo." Then you pointed your wand to wherever you wanted the object to go. "Oh, but look at this spell!" Cat murmured, turning over the page. "Magic Dictation" it was called. She studied the instructions. "Have a pen ready beside a piece of paper. Wave your wand and say the command, Squiggleypaparady, then begin to dictate in a loud, clear voice." Cat giggled. How did witches ever manage to learn all these complicated words? "Swiggly, I mean squiggley, squiggleypaparady," Cat whispered, struggling to get the sounds right.

"Oh, I just have to try this!" She was gripping the wand in her pocket so hard there were marks dug into her left hand, and an idea occurred to Cat. Why couldn't she do her homework and practice a little spell at the same time? It made perfect sense, didn't it? "And I have so many things I want to write down," Cat said out loud. "It will be much faster this way."

Opening her journal at a clean page, Cat positioned her purple pen beside it. She loved being allowed to write in purple ink, just like the girls at Ruthersfield did. Her teacher didn't mind, just as long as her handwriting was neat and her spelling correct. Cat strained her ears, making sure she could still hear opera music coming from the kitchen, which her mother and Marie Claire always listened to while they got the bread doughs started for the next day. It would not be good if Poppy chose this moment to come in and say good night. "Okay," Cat whispered, feeling her excitement start to build. She flexed her fingers and picked up her wand, making sure she was holding it the right way. Then, waving the wand in the air, Cat carefully pronounced the word, "Squiggleypaparady!"

The pen stood up, twitched, and flopped down again, knocking its lid on the desk a few times. "Oh, I left the top on!" Cat giggled. "Silly me." Leaning over the desk, she pulled the lid off and repeated the spell. This time she watched in amazement as the pen twitched and stood up. Cat squealed, covering her mouth with her hand. This was unbelievable. The pen hovered over the page, and Cat realized it was waiting for her to speak.

"Ahh . . . Antonia Bigglesmith got a toy airplane for her fourth birthday and told her parents right then that she was going to fly one herself one day." The pen scrawled away across the page, and Cat felt a great wave of pride sweep over her. She had done it! The spell was working correctly.

"When she was six," Cat continued, "she went for a—Hey, stop!" Cat yelled as the pen lurched off the page and started scribbling on the desk. She launched forward and tried to grab it, but the pen darted away and drew a squiggly line on the wall. "Stop that!" Cat shouted, and the pen wrote "Stop that."

"Get back on my journal! Flipping fish cakes!" Cat gasped, chasing after the pen. "Get back on my journal! Flipping fish cakes!" the pen scribbled in large, loopy purple script.

"Mamma is going to have a fit," Cat groaned, and the pen scrawled her words right across the ceiling. Trying not to say another word, Cat watched her pen hover in the air for a few moments, as if it was waiting for her to speak. Then, looking for something new to draw on, it dived to the floor, where it stared to draw circles.

"Got you," Cat panted, stomping on it quickly with her foot. She stamped as hard as she could, crushing purple ink all over the wooden boards. Cat cleaned up the mess with a handful of tissues and then moved her rug with the ducks on it, the one Auntie Charlie had made her, over the purple stain. Looking around at the walls and ceiling, Cat gave a soft groan. She would have to scrub the rest of the pen off tomorrow, when she didn't feel quite so tired. At least it was meant to be washable.

But Cat couldn't help smiling as she picked up her journal, because there, at the top of the page, was one perfect line of magic writing. Cat admired it for a while before slipping the journal into her backpack. Her eyes were sore, and she couldn't stay awake any longer. She would just have to finish her homework on the bus.

As Cat lay in bed with the lights out she could hear her jacket occasionally knocking against the inside of the cupboard. Soft, muffled thuds as it waved the sleeves about. But it wasn't a sound that she minded. In fact, it made Cat smile because it reminded her, as she drifted off to sleep, that she had finally got her most cherished wish. She had inherited the gift of magic.

Chapter Six

....

Maxine Gibbons and Her Big Mouth

"YOU LOOK TIRED," POPPY REMARKED AS CAT PADDED into the kitchen the next morning. Marie Claire's favorite opera station was playing on the radio, and a fire crackled in the hearth. There was a sweet smell of caramelized fruit in the air.

"I got to sleep a bit late," Cat admitted, smiling at her mother. Cat loved the coziness of the bakery, the warmth and the happiness that surrounded her, and she had a sudden hopeful feeling that everything would be all right. There wasn't time now, but she would tell her mother as soon as the bakery closed this afternoon.

"I made raspberry muffins," Poppy said, offering the

plate to Cat. Her long braid dangled over her shoulder, the ends streaked with flour.

"No thanks, Mamma." Cat opened the freezer. She dug about for the box of toaster tarts and took out two cardboard-looking squares. "I know, but I like them," Cat said, before Poppy had even commented.

"Fake, artificial, and disgusting." Poppy shuddered, although she didn't really look mad. "I don't know why I even allow them in the house."

"Because I'm your daughter and you love me," Cat said, popping them into the toaster.

"It is funny the way life works," Marie Claire mused, arranging croissants on a tray. "Your mother loves to bake, Cat, and you, who grew up in a bakery, have no interest whatsoever and would rather eat these toaster tart things!"

"Cat doesn't have to be like me," Poppy said. "She'll probably end up flying airplanes like Antonia Bigglesmith!" She smiled at Cat. "Honestly, I don't mind what you do as long as you're happy."

"Oh, Mamma, thank you for saying that." Cat wrapped her toaster tarts in a napkin. Perhaps telling her mother wasn't going to be so hard after all. "Sorry to rush, but I'll miss the bus if I don't hurry."

"Don't forget your jacket," Poppy said, which Cat had every intention of doing. It was still twitching about in her cupboard, although the magic seemed to be wearing off. Luckily she had an extra pair of gloves and an old scarf she could put on since her others had escaped through the window.

"I'm really not cold, Mamma."

"You shouldn't run and eat at the same time," Marie Claire called after her. "It is not good for the digestion."

But Cat didn't hear. She was already out the back door, leaving the warm, muffin-scented kitchen behind. Sprinting up the canal path, Cat arrived at the bus stop at exactly the same time as the bus. She clambered on, out of breath, and was about to sit down next to her friend Anika Kamal, when she saw Peter waving at her, pointing to the seat beside him. Cat hesitated a moment. She looked at Anika and shrugged, then moved down the aisle toward him.

"What is it?" Cat said. "Why aren't you back there with your brainy friends?"

"Have you told your mum yet?" Peter asked, launching right in. "Because I've been thinking about it, Cat, and I don't trust you. You're going to get yourself into trouble."

"That's not a very nice thing to say," Cat replied. "Anyway, I'm going to tell her after school. I promise."

"So you haven't tried any more spells?"

"Not really." Cat scratched her nose, staring past Peter out the window.

"You're completely fibbing, Cat. I can always tell because you scratch your nose and won't look at me."

"And you are so annoying!" Cat snapped. "Thinking you know everything."

As the bus turned down Glover Lane, Cat said, "Oh, Peter, please shift over. Can I sit by the window?" Not giving him time to answer, Cat clambered across Peter's long legs, squishing herself into his seat and forcing him to change places. She pressed her face against the glass just as the bus rumbled past the large gray stone building of Ruthersfield Academy. "They look so graceful, don't they?" She sighed, watching flocks of girls swoop down on their broomsticks. "Just like big, purple swans. Oh, there's Clara Bell!" Cat shrieked, banging on the glass as the magical history teacher landed outside the school gates. Cat yanked open the window and stuck her head out, waving madly. "Hello, Ms. Bell!" Cat shouted, causing most of the girls to turn and look. She couldn't wait to tell her she was a Late Bloomer too! Holding on to her hat, Ms. Bell waved back, her curls blowing about in the wind. "Oh, she sees me, she sees me," Cat squealed, paying no attention to the snickering Ruthersfield students pointing in her direction.

Cat turned to Peter, her eyes all aglow, forgetting she meant to be mad at him. "Just think, Peter. I could be flying to school next year. Flying on an actual broomstick!"

Cat was so eager to get home that afternoon she ran the whole way, not bothering to wait for the bus. A waft of curry scent hit her as she jogged past the Indian restaurant Anika's parents owned, and Mrs. Kamal waved to Cat through the window. As she raced down the canal path a light fog hung over the water, and the air was as cold as a glass of lemonade. She would tell her mother right away if there weren't any customers in the bakery. But when Cat pushed open the door, the shop was crowded with people, which often happened when the weather turned cold. Throwing her backpack down behind the counter, Cat put on an apron and immediately started to help. The air was warm and spicy with the scent of gingerbread. Poppy only made it during the month of November, and even though Cat didn't like to eat it, she loved the way it smelled.

"Yes, Maxine, what can I get you?" Cat said, smiling at Maxine Gibbons. Nothing could spoil her good mood today, and Cat held her secret close. She was filled with kindness toward everyone, even horrible, mean-mouthed Maxine.

"You're in a good mood, Cat," Maxine said, staring at her suspiciously. She patted a hand over her pink chiffon head scarf, which covered the rows of tight curlers Maxine never seemed to take out.

"It's a beautiful day," Cat replied, pulling her sweater down over the magic wand.

"Mmm, if you say so. I think it's freezing cold and miserable." Maxine sniffed. "I'll have a white crusty loaf and an éclair. One of those nice big ones with lots of cream in them." She turned away and immediately started talking to Mrs. Plunket, from the post office.

"Please," Cat whispered under her breath, reaching for a paper bag and wondering if Maxine would ever learn some manners. Crouching down behind the counter because the éclairs were on the bottom shelf, Cat could feel the magic wand pressing against her leg. She glanced around, but no one could see her back here. The wand had been in her pocket all day and she hadn't touched it once, although she'd been tempted during lunch and recess. Now, just meaning to hold it for a second, Cat slid the wand free. Then, before she could stop herself, she pointed it at an éclair and whispered the word, "Aloftdisimo!" Cat had been thinking about this spell since breakfast, wanting to try it out. It had looked so easy in the book, a tiny, little, move an object spell, and even though she had a strong feeling this probably wasn't a good idea, Cat simply couldn't resist. Her arm started to tingle, and the fizzy feeling shot through her body. She held up the paper bag and pointed the wand at it. "In there, please," Cat whispered, watching the éclair rise. It flew into the bag, and Cat twisted the paper shut, giving a soft squeal of delight. She scrambled to her feet and handed the bag to Maxine, beaming with pride. "Here you go," Cat said. "One éclair!"

"Better be a nice one," Maxine snapped, as the bag crackled open and the éclair floated out. "What in heaven . . . ," she shrieked, grabbing on to Mrs. Plunket's arm. "Did you see that?" Maxine spluttered, watching the éclair fly around the bakery. "What on earth did that girl just do?"

A collective gasp rose up from the customers because the éclair was now hovering near the ceiling, as if it were a giant, cream-stuffed bee.

"I've got chills," Maxine said, her head tilted upward and her mouth gaping open. "A flying cream cake is not normal! You know what this means, don't you?"

Cat was frozen behind the counter. She couldn't bear to watch, but it was impossible to look away as the éclair swooped down, plunging right into Maxine's mouth. There was a long moment of absolute silence, and then everyone started talking at once. Everyone except for Maxine, who couldn't speak, and her mother, Cat noticed, who was holding on to the counter so tightly her knuckles had turned white.

It was Marie Claire who took charge, walking over to Maxine and calmly handing her a tea towel. "Wipe yourself off with this," she said, although Maxine seemed to be doing an excellent job gobbling up the éclair.

"If I hadn't seen it myself I would not have believed it," Maxine exclaimed, licking cream from around her mouth. She dabbed at her face with the tea towel, although there wasn't much left to wipe up. Her small eyes sparkled with relish as she turned toward Poppy. "That daughter of yours has got the gift!"

Cat's mother didn't answer. She was staring at Cat in disbelief. Disbelief that was rapidly changing to horror. "Where did you get that?" Poppy croaked, noticing the wand in Cat's hand.

"I . . . I found it yesterday in Gran and Grandpa's attic," Cat whispered. "That's when I realized I'd got the gene. I wanted to tell you, but I know how you feel about magic and I was scared you might be mad." Cat's face flushed with heat.

Maxine gave Mrs. Plunket a knowing look. "I can't wait to tell her grandparents about this! Oh, my goodness, I just can't!"

"But . . . but . . ." Poppy shook her head. "You're eleven years old, Cat. That's far too late for magic to show up. I was only a baby," she whispered, covering her face with her hands. "This cannot be happening."

"Oh, it most definitely is happening," Maxine said firmly.

"Mamma, Ruthersfield Academy has a special entrance exam for Late Bloomers," Cat rushed on, deciding that she might as well get this over with now. "I've been reading all about it, and I really, really want to try out for a place." Her mother didn't answer.

"It's not as fancy as the seven-plus examination," Maxine whispered to Mrs. Plunket in her not so quiet voice. Seven was the age most girls started attending Ruthersfield Academy. "Not that they'd take Cat anyway," she continued. "Not after what happened."

"Mamma?" Cat said. Her mother's lip had started to tremble, and Cat suddenly felt nervous. The shop had gone silent again, but none of the customers were leaving.

"No." Poppy shook her head, twisting the dishcloth round her hands. "No," she said again. "You cannot try out for Ruthersfield."

Cat's mouth went dry. "Mamma, how can you say that? This is my dream. You know I've always longed to be magic." She stared at her mother. "And I'm happy," Cat said. "I've never been so happy. You told me this morning that's what mattered. I could do whatever I wanted with my life as long as it made me happy."

"But not magic," Poppy whispered. "You know I didn't mean magic."

"But why?" Cat said in frustration. "Why do you hate magic so much? You never talk about it, Mamma." She took a deep, shaky breath. "You chose not to be a witch. Isn't that why you dropped out of Ruthersfield? You liked making cakes instead of magic?"

"It's not that simple, Cat." Poppy shook her head again. "You don't understand. And the answer's still no."

"Please," Cat said, turning to Marie Claire. "Tell her, Marie Claire. It's my choice."

"I do think Cat has a point," Marie Claire said quietly.

"I don't want to talk about this now," Poppy said, glancing at her customers. "There are people here waiting to buy things."

"I think it's about time Poppy told Cat the truth," Maxine murmured to Mrs. Plunket. "We've all held our tongues for too long."

"What truth?" Cat looked from Maxine to her mother. "What does she mean, Mamma?"

"Maxine Gibbons, this is not your business," Poppy snapped, her face drained of color. She sniffed the air. "I smell gingerbread burning." And without meeting Cat's gaze, she hurried through to the kitchen.

"What is it?" Cat said, turning to Maxine.

Maxine moistened her lips, and Mrs. Plunket put a hand on her arm. "Best not to say anything, Maxine."

"Please don't," Marie Claire said rather fiercely, and all the customers murmured their agreement.

Maxine's cheeks puffed. Her lips quivered and her nose twitched. She looked as if she were about to explode. "Your mother didn't drop out of Ruthersfield," she burst out. "Poppy was expelled. Expelled for doing something so dreadful it still makes my blood run cold when I think about it." Maxine's words gathered speed like a snowball rolling down a hill. "She turned her own parents to stone. Left them standing outside in the cold for years." Maxine rolled her eyes skyward. "Poor Edith and Roger! Can't imagine what that must have been like for them. And it wasn't just her parents either. Your mother went around town turning everything to stone. Animals, birds, policemen. Poppy was crazed, out of control. None of us were safe in our beds. We were all so petrified. I didn't sleep a wink for nights on end. Ohh, it was terrifying." Maxine's eyes gleamed with the sheer delight of telling. "I've always thought it was wrong to keep that from you," she added.

Cat stared at Maxine, a sick, clamminess creeping over her.

"Great job, Maxine!" Ted Roberts, the postman,

remarked, giving Cat a sympathetic look. "I'm sure Poppy would be proud of the way you handled that."

"Well!" Maxine fiddled with the collar of her coat. "Cat was going to find out sooner or later."

"And how lovely it came from you!" Ted Roberts said sharply. "You take everything that woman says with a grain of salt, Cat. This town adores your mother. And none of us are perfect, are we? We've all done things we're ashamed of."

"Indeed we have," Marie Claire said, giving Maxine a pointed look. "Now, isn't it time for you to be on your way, Maxine Gibbons?"

"Well," Maxine said with a sniff. "If that's all the thanks I get for being honest . . ." And she marched toward the door.

"Wait!" Cat called after her, suddenly finding her voice. "I don't believe a word of it, Maxine. My mother's a wonderful person. She would never do any of those things." As Maxine banged the door shut behind her, Cat shouted out, "You're a horrible old bat."

"Honestly," Marie Claire grumbled, wrapping an arm around Cat's waist. "If I had the strength, I'd push that woman into the canal."

"We'd all help," Ted Roberts agreed.

"She's nothing but an old gossip," Marie Claire said.

"Your mother doesn't have an evil bone in her body."

"So it's not true, then?" Cat questioned. "About Mamma turning my grandparents to stone?"

Throwing Cat looks of support, the villagers filed out of the shop. When the last customer had gone, Marie Claire sighed and said, "It all happened a long time ago."

"Oh, my gosh!" Cat put a hand over her mouth. She thought she might be sick. "I don't believe it! How could she do that?" And all of a sudden, the person Cat thought she knew better than anyone else in the world wasn't the same person at all. "I always knew Mamma didn't want me to get the magic gene. And now I know why."

"Will you calm down and listen, Cat Campbell? Poppy didn't suddenly go crazy. Things had been building for a long time. Your mother hated magic. Really hated it. Baking was her passion, even then. She was miserable at Ruthersfield, but your grandparents forced her to stay there. And they refused to let her bake."

"That doesn't sound at all like Granny and Grandpa," Cat said. "They're so proud of Mamma for winning all her Young Baker of the Year awards."

"They are now. Things were different back then," Marie Claire explained soberly. "Your mother kept trying to tell them how sad she was, but they wouldn't listen to her."

"So she turned them to stone?"

"Not on purpose, of course." Marie Claire sounded so calm and matter-of-fact. "Her emotions got out of hand and so did her magic. It really wasn't Poppy's fault."

Cat was silent for a long moment, her own feelings a tangled mess. "I just can't believe it," she said at last. "It seems so unlike Mamma. I wish Maxine had never told me." And then rather more glumly, Cat said, "She's never going to let me try out for Ruthersfield, is she? Not with a past like that."

Chapter Seven

....

No Means No

WANTING TO BE ALONE, CAT HURRIED UPSTAIRS TO her room. For the first time in her life the bakery did not smell comforting, and Cat breathed in the stench of burnt gingerbread, feeling smothered by its scorched sugar tang. Lying down on her bed, she pressed her face into a pillow, wishing the things she had just heard were not true. A flurry of emotions swirled through her, and she ached for the solid, comforting presence of her dad. Cat had never felt so alone in her life. It all made sense now, why her mother hated magic so much.

"Cat?" Poppy knocked on Cat's bedroom door. "Can I come in?"

Cat lifted her head up as her mother opened the door a crack. "I brought you some fresh gingerbread. The last lot wasn't even fit for the birds."

"Mamma, why didn't you tell me?" Cat burst out, feeling light-headed and dizzy. "I can't believe I had to hear it from Maxine."

"Oh, Cat, I'm so sorry," Poppy said. She walked into the room and put a plate of warm gingerbread and a glass of milk down on Cat's nightstand. Sitting beside her, Poppy leaned over and gave Cat a long hug.

"You should have told me, Mamma," Cat murmured.

Poppy sighed. "It's not an easy thing to talk about, especially since you've always loved magic so much. I was worried you wouldn't understand. And you have such a special relationship with your grandparents, Cat. I didn't want to ruin that. Besides," Poppy added, "I was ashamed of what I'd done, and I was scared you'd think badly of me. Sometimes sadness and anger can make a person do terrible things."

"Why did Granny and Grandpa care so much about magic?" Cat asked her.

"It meant everything to them, the fact that I'd got the gift like Great-Granny Mabel." Poppy sighed again. "And then when I didn't want to do magic, well, they just couldn't accept it. I was such a disappointment to them."

"Oh, Mamma." Cat clambered onto her mother's knee. She was so tall now, her feet touched the floor, but Cat didn't care. She loved the warmth her mother gave off, as if she had just stepped out of the oven, and the way her long dark braid always smelled of cake batter. "It's okay," Cat said, staring out the window. After a moment she asked, "Why didn't you get sent to Scrubs Prison? Isn't that where evil witches go? How come it ended up all right?"

"Because of Auntie Charlie and Marie Claire," Poppy said. "You know Marie Claire has always been like a second mother to me, and I couldn't wish for a better friend than Charlie." She gave a fond smile. "They helped bring me back from the dark side. I had lost my passion for baking, you see. Without it I was bitter and sad. But as soon as I stopped being angry and starting baking, all the things I had turned to stone changed back again." Poppy paused for a moment. "It took your grandparents a little longer than everyone else to turn back. I think they weren't ready to accept me for who I was, but once they came around, the spell wore off, and they've been great ever since. Well, your grandmother still drives me up the wall sometimes, but no more than anyone else's mother."

"Does Dad know?"

"He does," Poppy said. "We have no secrets from each other. Anyway, it all happened a long time ago, and I don't like thinking about it. Which is why this has taken me off guard, Cat." Poppy's voice grew serious. "I wasn't expecting you to get the gift, not after eleven years."

"Nor was I," Cat agreed. "But I'm so happy, Mamma; you've no idea!"

"So what happened," Poppy asked, "in the attic?"

Cat sensed her mother didn't really want to hear, and as Cat told her about the spider changing color, she could feel her mother's body stiffen.

"You should have told me yesterday, Cat. Honestly, I can't believe your grandparents let you take my old wand! What were they thinking?"

"Mamma, don't blame Gran and Grandpa. It wasn't their fault. They didn't know I took it," Cat said.

"Well, they'll know soon enough from Maxine."

"I wasn't trying to hide it from you, either," Cat explained. "I just didn't want to make you mad. Plus," Cat admitted, "I was scared of telling you because I thought you might not let me apply to Ruthersfield."

Poppy shuddered. "I can't imagine having anything

to do with Ruthersfield Academy ever again." The force of her words shocked Cat, and she slid off her mother's knee.

A knocking sound came from inside Cat's cupboard, and Poppy started, turning to look. "Cat!" she gasped loudly, suddenly noticing the wall behind her. "'Flipping fish cakes!'" she read. "What on earth?" Poppy stood up. "I can't believe you did this. Why in heavens would you write on the walls?"

"It wasn't me," Cat tried to explain, hoping her mother wouldn't look up, because "Mamma is going to have a fit" was still scrawled across the ceiling in loopy purple script.

"Then who exactly was it, Cat? Because I will be calling his parents right now."

"No, Mamma, you don't understand," Cat said, sensing this wasn't going to end well. "I tried to make my pen write on its own last night, and it got a bit carried away."

"You've been practicing magic up here?" Poppy put her hands on her hips and tossed her braid over her shoulder. "Seriously, Cat, I don't believe this."

"I'm really sorry. It's washable ink. I'll clean it up, I promise."

"And what's in the cupboard?" Poppy said, as another muffled thud came from inside.

"Clothes, Mamma, that's all."

"Really!" Poppy looked like she didn't believe a word of it. "Let's see, shall we?" And marching over, she flung open the cupboard door. Cat's white winter jacket flapped out, waving its arms about and flopping across the floor like a giant puffy ray. It was considerably calmer than the last time Cat saw it, and she gave a sigh of relief.

"You should have seen my jacket yesterday, Mamma. It was really out of control."

"This whole thing is out of control," Poppy said, holding out her hand. "You have no idea what you're doing, Cat. I need you to give me the wand."

"Mamma, no! Please, please, please don't take my wand."

"Magic isn't a game, Cat. Now give me the wand before someone gets hurt."

"But will you let me try out for Ruthersfield?" Cat pleaded. "I know I can get better if I practice and take lessons."

"Cat, I'm sorry. This affects the whole family. The answer's still no." Poppy stepped toward her daughter and gently took the wand from Cat's hand. "I know this seems tough to you right now, but one day you'll understand." She shoved the wand in her apron pocket as if she couldn't bear to touch it, and her voice grew tight. "I will not have magic in this house."

"You're taking away my dream, Mamma."

"Oh, Cat," Poppy murmured, opening her arms wide. But Cat stepped away. She didn't feel like being hugged right now.

Chapter Eight

Peter Helps Out

CAT HAD HOPED HER MOTHER MIGHT HAVE RECONSID-
ered overnight, but she knew as soon as she
entered the kitchen the next morning that nothing
had changed. *Le Nozze di Figaro*, one of Marie Claire's
favorite operas, was playing loudly, while Poppy
stood over a tray of cupcakes, piping swirls of creamy
frosting on top. Her body looked stiff, as if she was
holding herself tight, and she worked with a fierce
intensity. Marie Claire sat at the table with her chin
in her hands, staring out the window, and Cat got
the feeling they had been discussing her. She helped
herself to a bowl of cereal, ignoring the fresh muffins

and croissants, and sat down beside Marie Claire.

"I'm sorry," Marie Claire murmured. She patted Cat's hand and whispered, "Give your mother time, Cat. This is hard for her. It is bringing back memories she would rather forget."

As soon as Cat got on the bus, she could tell that most of the kids already knew what had happened in the bakery the day before. They were whispering and pointing as she walked down the aisle, and Cat was surprised to see Anika sitting next to Karen Miller. Anika always saved the seat beside her for Cat.

"I'm sorry," Anika said, fiddling with a strap on her backpack. "My mum's a bit worried about me, you know, getting too close to you at the moment."

"Why?" Cat said, hovering in the aisle.

"Sit down," the bus driver shouted, and Cat took the empty seat opposite.

"Why?" she said again, leaning over toward Anika.

"Because you've got the magic gene," Karen Miller announced. "Maxine Gibbons told my mum."

"I'll bet she told everyone's mum," Cat muttered.

"It's just that my parents are a little afraid," Anika said. "They think because you attacked Maxine with a flying éclair, you might do something to us."

"But I didn't attack her," Cat said. "Well, not on purpose. I was just trying to move the éclair with my wand, you see, and the spell went a bit out of control."

"I think that's why they're worried," Anika explained. "My dad started going on about Madeline Reynolds, and how out of control she was and how nobody saw it coming. And Maxine told us all about the stuff your mum did when she was at Ruthersfield, and well, they're concerned that . . ." Anika trailed off, staring at her backpack.

"Both of our mums are worried you might flip out and turn us to stone or something," Karen finished for her.

"You know I would never do that," Cat said. Her throat had gone tight, and she pulled a tissue out of her pocket and blew her nose hard, not wanting to cry on the bus.

"I know you wouldn't," Anika agreed, looking uncomfortable. "It's just best we don't sit together for a few days, that's all. My mum will come round."

Cat nodded and stared out the window, shutting her eyes as they drove past Ruthersfield. She couldn't bear to look at the academy this morning. The seat creaked and Cat felt someone sit down beside her. She turned to see Peter squeezing his long, cricketlike legs into the narrow space between them. Occasionally, like right now, the sight of Peter Parker was as comforting as a pair of flannel pajamas.

"Why did you move?" Cat said, shifting over.

Peter shrugged. "Just felt like it."

"Well, thanks. That was nice."

"And I thought you might like to try out my walkie-talkies with me." Peter pulled one of the handsets from his backpack and gave it to Cat. It had a little metal box attached to the middle with a great deal of rubber bands. "That's the booster box I made," Peter said. "To get better range."

"Why aren't you doing this with Adam?" Cat said suspiciously. Adam and Peter were in the science club together, and it had been Adam who had helped Peter with his asteroid calculations. "I'm sure Adam would love to play walkie-talkies with you."

"Look, Mum thought you might have a hard time at school today, so I'm trying to be nice, that's all."

Cat examined the walkie-talkie. "You don't need to be kind to me, Peter, just because Auntie Charlie says so."

"You're right, I don't. So do you want to keep the walkie-talkie or not?"

"Thank you," Cat said, managing a small smile. "They look fun. We can try them out after school."

Peter demonstrated how the receiver worked, flipping the on-off switch and the button to press when you talked. It was only as they neared Potts Bottom Elementary that he brought up the subject of yesterday.

"So, that must have been pretty hilarious," Peter said. "Seeing Maxine get hit in the face with an éclair! Your mum told my mum all about it."

"I would have done it deliberately if I'd known how," Cat muttered. "It was pretty funny though!" Keeping her voice low because she didn't want Anika and Karen to hear, Cat whispered, "So you heard what Maxine said about my mother, then?"

"I did, but only because my mum wanted me to know the true story and not Maxine's version."

"Are you surprised?" Cat whispered.

"Not really. It was a long time ago, and Mum said she didn't blame Auntie Poppy one bit for what happened." Peter shrugged. "Don't forget, I've grown up with your mother, Cat. She's one of the nicest people I know, as well as being the best baker."

"Except she's not going to let me apply to Ruthersfield," Cat said, embarrassed to hear her voice wobbling. "She even took the wand away so I can't practice anymore."

"Cat, I'm really sorry," Peter said, and he did sound sorry. "I know how much you wanted this."

Cat nodded, not trusting her voice.

"Look, I'll ask my mum to talk to Auntie Poppy if you like. If anyone can convince her, my mum can."

"Oh, would you?" Cat cried out, not even caring that

Anika and Karen were staring at them. "That would be utterly brilliant!"

The Potts Bottom Elementary School was a new, airy building, full of windows and natural light. The old redbrick structure with its gloomy interior and cracked slate roof had been knocked down two years ago. When Cat walked in, most of the kids avoided talking to her or even looking at her, as if she had a strange, contagious disease. She was the only person left without a partner in science class, so she had to join Anika and Karen as a threesome. But every time her hand touched Karen's, Karen pulled away quickly with a little gasp.

"Look, I don't even have a wand on me," Cat snapped at one point. "So you can relax, okay? I'm not going to put a hex on you."

Karen and Anika had laughed nervously at this, but they both looked terrified. At lunchtime no one would sit at her table, and she couldn't eat with Peter because he had raced off to science club. During recess Cat wandered around by herself, not knowing whom to talk to. It was a huge relief when the day finally ended.

"How was school?" Marie Claire asked when Cat got home. She had come in through the kitchen door so she wouldn't have to see her mother in the bakery.

"About a zero," Cat said, hugging Marie Claire and going straight upstairs to her room. She found her jacket nestled in a corner, and every few seconds it would puff up and down as if it were lightly breathing. Cat knew she should scrub the pen off her walls, but instead she ate three Twirlie bars and finished up her essay on Antonia Bigglesmith, wearing the furry pilot's cap for inspiration as she wrote. She was just checking through her paper for spelling mistakes (which she would normally have asked her mother to do) when Peter's voice came crackling out of her backpack. "Cat Campbell, come in. Do you read me, Cat Campbell?"

Cat pulled out the walkie-talkie and pressed the green talk button. "I can hear you, Peter Parker. Loud and clear! Wow, these work really well!"

"Mission accomplished on my end," Peter said. "Just wanted to let you know."

"Peter, please talk in English. We're not spies, okay? What mission are you talking about?"

"I spoke to my mum and she's on her way over to see your mum right now."

"What did she say?" Cat asked, pulling off the cap and scratching her head. "Gosh, I'm so nervous, Peter!"

"Let me put it this way: She's in one of her determined moods!"

Cat had to smile at this because Auntie Charlie was

the most determined person she knew. Not that you would ever guess this if you saw her. She was the same height as Cat, with frizzy blond hair and a wide, gap-toothed smile. She had freckles all over her face, and even though she was thirty-six years old, she often got mistaken for a schoolkid.

"I'll let you know how it goes," Cat said, wondering how she was going to survive the wait.

There was only one thing to do when Cat felt this nervous. She curled up on the floor of her cupboard, taking her jacket in with her for company. It was soft and cuddly, and the gentle puffing movements made it feel more like a pet than a coat. Snuggled underneath it, Cat pulled the cupboard door almost shut, leaving a small opening to let in a little light and fresh air. She had no idea how long she'd been in there, but it felt like hours when Cat heard her mother's voice.

"Cat, where are you?" Poppy said.

Peeping through the crack, Cat could see her mother looking around the room. "Mamma?" Cat pushed open the cupboard door.

"What on earth are you doing in there?"

"Hiding. Peter told me Auntie Charlie was coming to see you."

"Ahhh!" Poppy walked over to the cupboard and

sat down on the floor. "So he told you she was going to try to change my mind, did he?"

Cat nodded, crunching up her hands and pressing her knuckles into her cheekbones.

"And you're wondering if I'm going to let you apply to Ruthersfield, are you?"

Cat nodded again, holding her breath.

"Well, Marie Claire pointed out that I was behaving just like my mother used to. But it took Auntie Charlie to convince me, which of course she did! So I'll call them tomorrow," Poppy said, putting Cat out of her misery. "There are no guarantees though," Poppy added as Cat screamed and rolled out of the cupboard into her mother's lap. "They don't take many girls your age. There are only a few places for Late Bloomers."

"I don't care, Mamma. You're the best!"

Poppy smiled, putting her arms around Cat's waist. "Charlie made me realize that I've got to let you apply because this is what you want. It's your dream, Cat, and however hard it is for me, I'm not going to stand in your way."

"Oh, Mamma, I love you, I love Auntie Charlie, I love everyone," Cat cried. "This is the happiest moment in my entire life so far. I get to try out for Ruthersfield!"

"But no more attempting spells until your interview," Poppy said. "Magic really can be dangerous, Cat, without proper supervision."

"Dad would be so happy, wouldn't he, Mamma?"

"Knowing your father, I believe he would be."

"I told him already," Cat confessed. "I wrote him a letter after I found out I was magic."

"Well, you know he'll come home when he can, then," Poppy said. "Now, how about you bring a bucket of hot soapy water up here and scrub those walls clean. Not sure how you're going to manage the ceiling though," she added, tilting her head back. "Didn't think I noticed that, did you?"

After her mother left, Cat picked up the walkie-talkie. "Peter Parker, Peter Parker, come in," she whispered, pressing the talk button. "Are you there, Peter Parker? Come in."

There was a loud crackling, and then Peter's voice came over the airwaves. "I hear you, Cat Campbell. What's the news?"

"News is good, Peter Parker," Cat said. She smiled at her handset. "News is really, really good."

"I worked out your odds," Peter told her. "You have about a one in eight hundred chance of getting in."

"Thanks, Peter. That makes me feel really confident!" Cat said, but not even terrible odds could dampen her mood. "And judging by your asteroid calculations, I'm not exactly worried."

"They have twelve places for the Late Bloomer class," Peter explained, sounding as if he were right there in the room with her. "And going by last year's numbers, two thousand and nineteen girls applied. So if you factor in the variables, like genetic strength from prior generations, strength of magic shown, et cetera, your odds come out to about one in eight hundred."

"Well, that's not so bad," Cat said hopefully. Now that she had her mother's support, Cat was certain she could conquer any challenge. And sitting still in her bedroom, she could almost feel her magic fizzing quietly inside her.

Chapter Nine

....

An Interview at Ruthersfield

THE MORNING OF HER RUTHERSFIELD INTERVIEW, CAT was too excited to eat breakfast. She skipped around the kitchen, glancing at the clock every few seconds and polishing the magic wand, which her mother had given back to her. "Is it time to go yet? I don't want to be late."

"You have a whole hour before you need to leave!" Poppy said. "Now, can you please sit still, Cat, because you're making me dizzy."

This was an impossible task, and Cat danced about until Marie Claire said, "All right, Cat. Let's go. I'm a slow walker. It will take us a while to get there."

"You look very smart," Poppy said, straightening her daughter's collar.

"I've got purple and gold socks on." Cat stuck out a leg. "Ruthersfield colors! Oh, I do hope they know how much I want to go."

"That will come across, I promise!" Poppy reassured her.

"I wish Dad was here for my interview. Don't you miss him too?"

"Every single day. But I keep reminding myself how happy he is. And I knew when I married him he'd be gone a lot."

"Then I wish you could take me to Ruthersfield," Cat said. "It seems so unfair. They won't let you bring your own daughter along to an interview."

Poppy turned away. She opened the fridge and closed it without removing anything. "I did ask, Cat, but Ms. Roach was firm. They have very strict rules for witches at the academy, and when I was expelled it was made quite clear to me that I'm not to step foot on Ruthersfield property ever again."

"But that was twenty-five years ago, Mamma."

"Twenty-seven," Poppy said. "But those are the rules, and we have to accept them."

"Well, I say it's stupid," Cat muttered.

"Yes, but I get the great pleasure of taking you,"

Marie Claire chimed in, slipping on her coat. Her fingers were often stiff in the mornings, and she struggled to do up her buttons. "I am looking forward to seeing inside the academy," she added, glancing over at Poppy. "It has always intrigued me, wanting to know what goes on in there."

"Me too," Cat agreed. She hugged her mother goodbye. "Wish me luck, Mamma."

"Luck," Poppy said, kissing the tip of her daughter's nose. "Just remember, Cat, Ruthersfield is intensely competitive. Don't be sad if this doesn't work out."

"And don't be sad if it does," Cat said.

Ruthersfield Academy was an imposing stone building that had always reminded Cat of a castle. She walked slowly up the wide stone steps, matching her pace to Marie Claire's. A rope bellpull dangled outside the front door, and Cat tugged on it, her stomach fluttering with nerves. After a few moments the double doors opened and a witch in a long purple cloak with gold braided trim stood there, her frizzy gray hair puffing out around her head like a mushroom cap. There was a rather awkward silence as the woman studied them.

"Hello," Cat said at last. "I'm Cat, I mean Catherine, Catherine Campbell." She stuck out her hand, wishing it wasn't so damp. "I've come for an interview."

"We are expected," Marie Claire added in her soft French accent.

"Ahhh." The woman held up a pair of glasses that were hanging on a chain around her neck and peered at Cat through them. "So you are Catherine Campbell." From the way she said this, Cat got the feeling that being Catherine Campbell wasn't exactly a positive thing.

"I am." Cat stood up straight. "And I'm really excited to be here. I'm a Late Bloomer."

"Well, you'd better come in," the woman said. "I'm Ms. Weedle, the spells and charms teacher here at Ruthersfield." She stared at Cat a few seconds longer before finally stepping aside. "Follow me, please. I'll take you straight to Ms. Roach. And do not open any doors or wander off. Stay right behind me."

Cat helped Marie Claire hobble inside. "It's so grand," Marie Claire murmured, looking around the entry hall.

"Look." Cat pointed to a crest hanging on the wall above the massive doors. It was the famous Ruthersfield crest, two crossed broomsticks over a cauldron. Underneath in cursive was written "Kibet fallow da." "I know what that means," Cat whispered. "Follow your passion! I read all about it in Mamma's old *History of Magic* book."

Ms. Weedle's face seemed to tighten and her lips

grew thin. "Come along," she instructed, leading the way down a long corridor.

Poor Marie Claire had trouble keeping up. Her ankle was swollen this morning, and she limped behind slowly. "Could we slow down, please?" Cat called out. "Marie Claire's foot is hurting her."

Ms. Weedle gave a brisk nod and abruptly slowed her pace, which Cat was glad about because it meant she could look around. One of the classroom doors was open, and Cat peeked inside, seeing rows and rows of girls waving magic wands about and chanting. They passed what looked like a chemistry lab, except clouds of purple smoke were billowing out of mini cauldrons and a number of toads were hopping around the room.

"Gosh, I love this place," Cat whispered to Marie Claire. "I just love everything about it."

"Oh, step close to the wall," Ms. Weedle said, speaking over her shoulder. "Here comes a beginner flying class." Cat stopped walking as a line of girls in their purple Ruthersfield uniforms wobbled by on broomsticks. An elegant young teacher led them, her long blond hair coiled into a twist, waving blood red nails in the air. "Stomachs in, shoulders back, girls. Good flying posture is essential." She glanced down the row of girls, like a competent mother duck. "Belinda, you are riding like a sack of potatoes."

"I'm sorry, Ms. Dancer," a girl in the middle said, gripping her broomstick for dear life. "I'm so scared I'm going to fall."

"You are two feet off the ground, Belinda. How on earth are you going to manage outside?"

As Cat watched them fly past, she felt an ache in her chest, wanting so much to join in. Oh, she would do anything to be swooping along behind those girls right now.

"Cat." Marie Claire touched Cat's arm lightly. "We must keep going."

Snapping out of her daydream, Cat followed Ms. Weedle, who kept glancing back at her, as if she might run off or do something unpredictable. The spells and charms teacher stopped in front of a padded, green leather door with a big brass knocker. "We're here," she said, sounding relieved. Ms. Weedle knocked once and turned the handle, ushering Marie Claire and Cat inside. A woman stood on a stepladder, filing purple folders of paperwork into a bookcase. She looked down at them, and Ms. Weedle said, "Could you tell Ms. Roach Catherine Campbell is here for her interview, please?"

"She's expecting you," the woman said, waving her free hand across the room to another door. "Go right on in."

Ms. Roach, the headmistress of Ruthersfield Academy, sat behind a huge walnut desk. She stood up as they came in. Cat tried to swallow down her nerves. A tall, thin woman with short gray hair and sharp blue eyes, Ms. Roach was an imposing figure. "Catherine Campbell," she said. "This is quite a surprise."

"A pleasant one, I hope," Marie Claire added in her gentle voice. "Cat is excited to be here."

"Is she now?" Ms. Roach stared so hard at Cat, Cat felt her face prickle with heat. "I have to admit I was a little taken aback when your mother called up requesting an interview for you. She tells me you have inherited the family magic gene."

Cat nodded, finding it difficult to speak with Ms. Roach studying her as if she were an insect under a microscope.

There was a soft knock on the door, and Ms. Roach called out, "Come in." Turning her head, Cat saw Clara Bell and another teacher enter the room. Clara Bell gave Cat a warm smile, and Cat immediately began to relax. She mouthed back an excited *Hello!*

Ms. Roach cleared her throat. "This is Ms. Bell, coordinator of the Late Bloomer's Program here at Ruthersfield, and Ms. Grendel, our magical management teacher. They are both on the committee for Late Bloomer applicants," Ms. Roach explained.

Marie Claire and Cat shook their hands. Ms. Grendel's shake was brisk and businesslike but Clara Bell took Cat's hand in both of hers and gave it a gentle squeeze.

"Just stay calm," she whispered, leaning forward so Cat could smell the faint scent of violets. "You'll be fine."

The teachers sat down beside Ms. Roach, and the headmistress motioned for Cat and Marie Claire to take the chairs opposite her desk. "So tell me what happened," Ms. Roach said to Cat. "How did this all begin?"

"Well . . ." Cat glanced at Clara Bell, who gave her an encouraging nod. "I was in my grandparents' attic and I found my mum's old novice wand." She wished her heart would stop racing, but Ms. Roach was about the most intimidating person she had ever met. "I was really excited because I've always loved magic. I've wanted to be a witch my whole life."

"Mmmmmm," Ms. Roach said, nodding. "Go on."

"Right. I waved it about and nothing happened, of course, and I was feeling a bit upset so I sat down on the floor, and that's when I felt a spider crawling on me. I really hate spiders! This one was huge. When I realized what it was, I screamed because I was so scared, and I flicked it with the wand. And then," Cat said breathlessly, breaking into a smile because she knew Ms. Roach was going to love this part, "then it changed colors, lots of colors, and it grew to the size of a golf ball. And when I waved my wand at it again, it started to bounce around the attic, as if it was made out of rubber."

"How thrilling for you," Clara Bell murmured. "That first magical moment!"

Ms. Roach just nodded, not looking particularly impressed. "So you were really frightened by the spider?" she confirmed, leaning forward slightly.

"I was," Cat admitted. "I was terrified."

"Mmmmm." It was a long drawn out "mmmmmmm." Ms. Roach made a steeple with her fingers and glanced at Ms. Grendel. "Which is when the magic happened?"

"Yes, yes, exactly," Cat said, shifting about in excitement.

"Mmmmm," Ms. Roach said again, tapping her nails on the table. "What are your thoughts, Ms. Grendel?"

The magical management teacher frowned. "A huge adrenaline rush brought on by fear can trigger a magical response in a carrier," Ms. Grendel said. "And once the magic has been activated this way, it will nearly always be out of control." She gave Cat a somber look. "There are things you can do, but this sort of magic is extremely difficult to manage. It's not very common, and when I do see magic like this, it's almost always in a Late Bloomer."

"That's why I want to come to Ruthersfield," Cat said. "So I can learn how to be a proper witch, just like my great-great-granny Mabel. She was brilliant."

"Indeed she was," Ms. Roach said. "Strong-willed to be sure, but one of our best head girls." She lowered her head for a moment. "Why don't we try a simple rolling spell, then?" Ms. Roach said, handing Cat a pencil. "This will show us how well you can handle your magic."

"No, no, not on the desk," Ms. Grendel broke in, waving her hands at Cat. "Do it on the rug over there, please."

"It will give you more space," Clara Bell said gently.

"Are you sure you can all see?" Cat said, placing the pencil on the edge of Ms. Roach's oriental carpet. "I don't want anyone to miss this."

"We can see just fine. Now, you have the wand with you, correct?" Ms. Roach said. Cat pulled it out of her pocket. "Okay, good. What I want you to do is wave it over the pencil and in a clear, calm voice say, "Rollypolumdum.""

"Okay." Cat nodded. Her heart was racing, and she wiped her hands down her skirt. "I'm a bit nervous," she admitted.

"Don't be. That will only make things worse," Ms. Grendel said.

"But nerves are quite normal," Clara Bell added. "Try to stay calm, Cat. Big, deep breaths. And you might want to turn your wand round the other way," she suggested gently.

"Oh!" Cat giggled. She flipped the wand around. "It's so hard to tell which end is which."

"It's slightly thicker at the handle end," Ms. Roach said. "A good witch can tell just by feel."

"Right." Cat stared at Ms. Roach. "Sorry," she whispered, "but what was that word again?"

"Rollypolumdum," the headmistress said.

Cat took a deep breath and waved her wand over the pencil. "Rollypolumdum," she cried, and the rug shot out from under Cat's feet, knocking her backward as it rolled across the floor. The teachers leapt out of their chairs.

"Oh, my goodness," Marie Claire said with a gasp. "What is happening?"

Cat scrambled to her knees in time to see the rug gather speed and roll up the pencil, a standing lamp, and all the furniture in its path. As it sped toward Ms. Roach's desk, Marie Claire tried to get out of the way but she couldn't move fast enough, and the rug grabbed her shoes and rolled up over her feet.

Ms. Roach waved her wand in the air. "Consticrabihaltus," she commanded, and the rug shuddered to a stop.

"Thank you," Marie Claire said, panting and resting a hand on her heart. "Cat gets a little overexcited, but she has such passion!"

"She certainly does," Clara Bell agreed. "And passion is so important for Late Bloomers."

Cat looked at Ms. Roach, trying to gauge her reaction. "My magic is powerful, isn't it?"

"Your magic is out of control," Ms. Roach said soberly. "Now if you could both step outside a moment, please, I'd like to talk things over with the committee." Clara Bell held up a pair of crossed fingers as Cat and Marie Claire left the room.

At least Cat knew she had someone on her side, but it was still complete torture waiting to be called back in again. They sat in the secretary's office, and Cat rocked back and forth on her chair, wondering how Marie Claire could remain so calm. The minutes ticked by and Marie Claire flipped through a Ruthersfield alumni magazine while Cat stared at Ms. Roach's door, desperate to know what they were saying about her.

When Ms. Grendel and Clara Bell finally came out, it was impossible to gauge anything from their faces. Before Cat could ask Clara Bell how it had gone, Ms. Roach appeared at the door, motioning them back into her office again. As soon as they were all seated, she let out a long breath.

"This was not an easy decision, Catherine." Ms. Roach picked up a piece of paper and studied it. "You know we have very few Late Bloomer places available."

"But I've definitely got the gift, haven't I?" Cat said.

"You do, but it's clearly a recessive gene and, because it was adrenaline triggered, almost impossible to control. Not like with your mother and Mabel Ratcliff, who were dominant carriers of the magic gene." Ms. Roach cleared her throat. "Ruthersfield does not have the resources to support your sort of magical ability, Catherine. You would need a one-on-one aide, constant monitoring, and the sort of special-needs help that Ruthersfield is not equipped to offer. We could not have you performing magic with the other girls." Ms. Roach shook her head. "It just isn't feasible, I'm afraid."

Cat felt like she was going to be sick. Her mouth had gone dry, and she twisted her fingers together.

"I am sorry to be so blunt," Ms. Roach said, "but I do feel that honesty is the best approach here."

"I'll work harder than anyone," Cat whispered, needing to make Ms. Roach understand.

"I'm sure you would. And Ms. Bell lobbied hard on your behalf." The headmistress's eyes filled with sympathy. "Unfortunately we can only take the best. Hard work and dedication are important, but so is your level of talent."

Cat felt as if she had been punched in the stomach.

"I'm very sorry, Catherine," Ms. Roach finished up softly, "but we will not be offering you a place."

"Please," Cat said, hating to beg but unable to stop herself. "Can't I even sit the exam?"

"I'm sorry." Ms. Roach shook her head.

"Come on, *chérie*." Marie Claire hoisted herself to her feet. "We appreciate your time, Ms. Roach. I am sure you must be very busy."

"Thank you for seeing me," Cat managed to say. She stood up and walked to the door, her arms wrapped around her stomach as if she could hold in her pain.

Cat walked quickly down the corridor, not waiting for Marie Claire. Some of the girls gave her curious looks as she passed, but she ignored them all. "That's Poppy Pendle's daughter," a girl with long ginger hair and freckles said, not even trying to keep her voice down. "I see her at the bakery all the time. What on earth is she doing here?"

"Who cares? She'll never come to Ruthersfield," her friend replied. "Ms. Roach wouldn't allow it."

Cat dug her nails into her palms, refusing to cry until she got outside. She pushed through the heavy front door and ran down the steps. With no one to see her, Cat let out a wail of sadness so raw and sharp it startled a black cat sitting nearby, and he ruffled his fur in distress. Sinking onto the bottom step, Cat buried her face in her hands. How could she tell her parents she had failed, and Auntie Charlie and Uncle Tom? Peter had been right about her odds, Cat realized. She had never really stood a chance.

"Cat," Marie Claire called out, limping her way slowly down the stairs. Cat couldn't answer. Her throat was too full of lumps. "You did the best you could. I'm proud of you." A deep shudder swept through Cat. She turned around and saw the pity in Marie Claire's eyes. "I know how much you wanted this," Marie Claire said.

"Even if I'd done the most amazing magic ever, I don't think Ms. Roach would have given me a place."

"How can you say that, *chérie*?"

"Because of what Mamma did. You saw how most of the teachers looked at me. And the girls. Ms. Roach doesn't want anything more to do with our family. She's scared I'll turn out like Mamma."

"You know this is not your mother's fault," Marie Claire said, putting a hand on Cat's shoulder.

Cat knew Marie Claire was right, but she also needed someone to be mad at. "I just wish Mamma hadn't done those things," she whispered.

"Come on, *chérie*, let's go home."

"Not right now. I can't. I want to see Granny and Grandpa." And Cat started to run. It hurt so much:

being given what she wanted more than anything else in the world, and then having it snatched away from her because she wasn't good enough. She'd never be good enough according to Ms. Roach.

Chapter Ten

....

Anywhere but Home

"CAN I STAY HERE TONIGHT?" CAT SAID, CURLED UP on her grandparents' sofa.

"You can't run away from your troubles, Cat," Grandpa Roger said, rubbing the arms of his chair.

"Oh, let her stay for the night," Granny Edith clucked, putting a cup of tea down beside Cat. "Just till she feels better. She's had quite a shock, not getting in to Ruthersfield. We all have," Edith added. "I can't pretend I'm not a little bit upset myself." She stroked a hand over Cat's hair. "I mean, if anyone should have been offered a place, it's our Kitty Cat."

Cat sipped her tea, glad that she hadn't gone

straight home. Granny Edith tucked a blanket around Cat's feet, and the soft murmur from the television was comforting, even though Cat wasn't used to watching it so early in the day. "Why didn't you ever tell me about Mamma?" she asked in a small voice. "About what she did to you both?"

"Old history," Grandpa Roger said sternly. "We all wanted to forget about it." He gave Granny Edith a hard look. "Maxine should never have told Cat."

"It just doesn't seem like Mamma," Cat said. She rubbed a corner of the blanket between her fingers. "Weren't you mad at her? How could you forgive her?"

"Poppy had every right to be furious with us," Grandpa Roger said. "We didn't listen to her, Cat. We did some things I really regret. I hate to say this, but we weren't good parents."

"Yes, we were," Granny Edith snapped back, taking Cat completely off guard. She had never heard her grandmother talk this way before. "We only wanted what was best for her."

"But we didn't listen to what Poppy wanted." Grandpa Roger looked serious. "You know we didn't, Edith. We messed up in a big way, and I don't blame her for turning us to stone."

Granny Edith fiddled with her wedding ring. "We made mistakes, I'll give you that," she muttered. "But things got out of hand." She drooped her head back against the sofa and closed her eyes for a moment. "I hate thinking about the past. Let's leave it at that."

All of a sudden her grandparents looked so sad and old that Cat leaned over and gave Granny Edith a kiss on the cheek. "You're both wonderful," she told them. "Best grandparents in the world!" Cat hesitated a moment, then said quietly, "I think Ms. Roach was worried my magic would get out of control like Mamma's did."

"Now, don't go blaming your mother because you didn't get a place," Grandpa Roger said. "Ms. Roach might be tough, but she's always been fair." He pushed himself to his feet. "Come on, Catkins. I'm taking you home."

Poppy was frosting cupcakes in the bakery kitchen, piping swirls of buttercream on top of buttery golden cakes. She put down her piping bag as Cat walked in holding on to her grandfather's hand.

"The wanderer returns," Grandpa Roger joked, picking up a little cake. "These look delicious, Poppy."

"Take some back to Mum," Poppy said, talking to her father but looking straight at Cat. "I'm so sorry it didn't work out, Cat. I know how much you wanted this." Poppy licked a blob of frosting off her finger. "If I could give you my magic gene, I would, willingly."

Cat nodded, finding it difficult to speak about what had happened. The hurt inside her was still too raw. "I know, Mamma." She turned to Marie Claire, who was sitting at the table sipping a cup of caffe latte. "I'm sorry I ran off, Marie Claire."

"That's all right, *chérie*. I quite understand," Marie Claire replied.

"I made your favorite cupcakes," Poppy said. "Vanilla with buttercream frosting."

"Thank you, but I'm not too hungry," Cat said, feeling as flat and deflated as a squashed balloon. "Maybe later. Right now I'd just like to be alone, if you don't mind."

Cat knelt on her bedroom floor and stared out the window. She had wanted to go to Ruthersfield so badly. Now she would have to stay at the elementary school with kids who were scared of her, worried she might go on a rampage and turn them all into stone. "And that's so silly," Cat whispered out loud. "Because I just want to be like Great-Great-Granny Mabel and make my family proud." Even Anika, her best friend, still wouldn't sit next to Cat on the bus. The only person she felt like seeing right now was Peter.

As soon as school got out, Cat packed up some cupcakes and walked over to Kettle Lane, where the

Parkers lived. She was grateful that her mother hadn't made her go back to school for the remainder of the day, because that would have been too awful to bear. During the summer months the flower beds surrounding the Parkers' cottage bloomed with roses and hollyhocks and blue waving lupines. Right now it looked a little bare, but a patch of bright pink cyclamen still offered some color. Auntie Charlie loved to garden. She also loved animals. The Parkers' goat bared its teeth at Cat as she walked up the path. Standing on the doorstep, Cat knocked a few times, waiting for someone to answer. Maybe Peter wasn't home yet, and knowing Auntie Charlie wouldn't mind if she waited inside, Cat pushed the door open. She stepped into the hallway and a trumpet sounded. "Intruder, intruder," a voice shouted. "Stop right there; put your hands in the air."

Cat dropped the cupcakes and flung her hands up as Peter came charging down the stairs.

"Yes!" He raised his fist. "It worked! My homemade burglar alarm!"

"Peter, that scared me half to death," Cat said.

"Which is just what it's meant to do. Look, I rigged up this wire under the rug, and when anyone steps over it, the alarm is triggered and the recording goes off. Adam did the voice for me."

"But I'm not a burglar, Peter."

"Well, I'm only going to set it at night, Cat. Duh!"

"I see." Cat picked up the cupcakes and burst into tears. "That's clever."

"Oh, Cat." Peter shuffled his feet uncomfortably. "I'm guessing it didn't go well."

"It was the opposite of well. It was awful, " Cat said, rubbing a sleeve across her eyes.

There was a slightly awkward silence. Finally Peter said, "Come and have a Twirlie bar, Cat. That always cheers you up."

The kitchen was warm and smelled of animals. Midas, the Parkers' Labrador, had just had a litter of puppies, and in the corner by the fire was a box with a sick goose in it. Auntie Charlie insisted that geese made the best pets, although by the look of things, this one didn't seem to be doing too well. A cage with two ginger-and-white guinea pigs sat on the counter, and Cat could hear them squeaking as she watched Peter root about in his backpack. After a great deal of hunting, he pulled out a rather squashed Twirlie bar. "Knew I had one in here somewhere."

"Thanks, Peter." Cat pulled off the wrapper and took a bite. "If you don't mind, I'd rather not talk. I just like being here."

"Fine with me," Peter said, starting on the cupcakes. "I really am sorry, Cat," he murmured at one point.

"I know." Cat sighed. "So am I."

They were sitting in silence when Auntie Charlie walked in from the garden, wearing a man's green jacket that was far too big for her, a basket of eggs in one hand. She took one look at Cat's face and hurried over to give her a hug. "Not good?"

"Not good," Cat agreed. "I'm trying to be brave, but it's difficult because I keep wanting to cry. So can we talk about other things?"

"Absolutely," Auntie Charlie said, putting the eggs into a wire basket. "Well," she said cheerfully, "my chickens are finally starting to lay. I think it was Marie Claire's music that did it. She lent me some opera, and the chickens really seem to like it."

"Hey, where's Dad?" Peter suddenly asked. "He's usually home by now."

"There's some sort of crisis going on down at the station," Auntie Charlie said. She picked up the goose and stroked him. "I'm not sure when Tom's going to be home."

"What sort of crisis?" Peter said in surprise. "Nothing exciting ever happens in Potts Bottom."

"I don't know." Auntie Charlie kissed the goose on its head. "I'm sure we'll find out soon enough."

Chapter Eleven

Don't Let Fear Stand in Your Way

I T WAS BEGINNING TO GET DARK AS CAT WALKED BACK home to the bakery. At the bottom of Peter's lane a small group of Ruthersfield girls flew past on their broomsticks, smells of beef stew wafting from the plastic shopping bags that dangled over each handle. Cat stopped for a moment, unable to drag her gaze away. She watched by the light of the street lamps as some of the girls swooped up and knocked on doors, delivering bags of stew to the occupants. They were like agile, graceful hummingbirds, and Cat gave a long shaky sigh, a lump forming in her throat. She was so caught up watching the girls that she didn't see Clara Bell land beside her until a soft hand touched her on the arm.

"I'm so sorry, Cat," Clara Bell said. "I did my best to convince Ms. Roach." She paused and then added, "I know how much magic means to you."

Cat nodded and tried to smile, but her mouth wouldn't keep still, and the smile wobbled away. "Ms. Roach told me I'd never be good enough, that my magic is too out of control." Cat stopped for a moment, trying to steady her voice. "That hurts. It really does, because I'm not ready to give up on being a witch."

"Then perhaps you should trust your instincts," Clara Bell said softly. She clapped her hands and raised her voice. "When you've finished your delivery, girls, you may go home."

"What are they doing?" Cat asked, blinking back tears.

"Community service. All our girls are expected to do it. This is the meals-on-broomsticks program for the elderly."

"It looks so fun," Cat said longingly. "I'd love to do that." She sniffed and wiped a hand across her nose. "But it's never going to happen now." The sound of the girls' laughter drifted toward them on the still air. Turning to Clara Bell, Cat said suddenly, "What did you mean? About trusting my instincts?"

"Well, if this feels like the right path for you, Cat,

then maybe you shouldn't give up just yet. You could always reapply next year. There are no rules to say that you can't."

"But Ms. Roach wouldn't take me," Cat said, staring at Clara Bell through the gloom. "She's already turned me down."

"Being a Late Bloomer is difficult. I should know. You have to work ten times harder than any other witch. It took me twice as long as most witches to get my magical degree, and later on I had to sit my teaching exam twice. I almost didn't take it after failing so badly the first time," Clara Bell confessed.

"Why did you?" Cat asked.

"Because I realized I could live with the failure of doing badly, but I couldn't live with the regret of not trying. And I'm so pleased I did, because even though I'll never be much of a potion mixer or crystal ball gazer, I love teaching magical history."

"Do you think I could really do it?" Cat said, a flutter of possibility in her stomach. "My magic is so hard to control."

"There are things you can do to practice," Clara Bell said, pulling a slim book out of her pocket. "This little volume, *The Late Bloomer's Guide to Magic*, was written many years ago by a wonderful witch, Francesca Fenwick, a Late Bloomer herself. There isn't much out there on the subject, I'm afraid, but I have always found reading this most useful and comforting. I keep it with me at all times. It is full of excellent advice for Late Bloomers, and if you take good care of it, I would be delighted to lend it to you." Clara Bell held the book out to Cat. It didn't weigh much and the cover was worn, but Cat knew that what she held was a treasure.

"Oh, Ms. Bell, thank you so much," Cat said, hardly noticing the Ruthersfield girls flying by on their way home. "I'll look after it, I promise."

"I know you will, Cat. And there are a few nice, simple spells at the back that you might want to try."

"I'm not the best at spells," Cat said, wincing at the memory of the pencil-rolling fiasco. "You've seen what happens, Ms. Bell."

"These ones are very manageable. There's a marvelous courage potion, but I'm afraid it calls for powdered griffin's tooth, which is almost impossible to come by nowadays. The Raising Your Spirits Cake is wonderful though. I still make it whenever I find myself flagging and in need of a little encouragement. You say a lovely, gentle chanting spell, and it only requires one magical ingredient, a puff of condensed dragon's breath. Most Late Bloomers can manage it. I know the recipe by heart. In fact," Clara Bell said, rooting around in her bag, "I just picked up some dragon's breath from the school supply store, so I'll give you a bottle if you like." She handed Cat a small purple glass vial. It didn't weigh much, and a thrill ran through Cat as she slid the little bottle into her pocket.

"Are you sure you can spare it, Ms. Bell?"

Clara Bell smiled. "They're running a two-for-one special on dragon's breath this week, so I got plenty." She touched Cat lightly on the arm. "Just remember," she said, "if you're not ready to give up on your magic, Cat, then maybe it's not ready to give up on you."

Cat held the book close. "I'm definitely not ready to give up on my magic. But I am scared," she admitted.

"And what exactly are you scared of?" Clara Bell asked.

"I'm scared of disappointing my mum because I know she doesn't want me to be a witch, and I'm scared of disappointing myself if I can't do it. And what if Ms. Roach is right and I'm not good enough? What if I'm never able to control my magic? What if I fail again and everyone laughs at me? I'm so scared of that happening."

"Cat," Clara Bell said, lifting Cat's chin up so she could look her directly in the eyes. "All these feelings are quite normal for the Late Bloomer. I'm not an expert on magic and I never will be, but there is one thing I've learned over the years that's been helpful.

It's an excellent piece of advice, and you'll find it on the first page of Francesca's book." Clara Bell paused a moment, and then said, "Nem zentar topello."

"What does that mean?" Cat said. "Nem zentar topello."

"It comes from the ancient language of witches, and it means 'Don't let fear stand in your way,' Cat Campbell."

"I'll try," Cat whispered, feeling braver than she had in a long time. Just standing beside Clara Bell gave her hope.

Chapter Twelve

·····················

The Late Bloomer's Guide to Magic

W HEN CAT GOT HOME SHE FOUND A POT OF HER favorite chicken noodle soup on the stove, the soup her mother always made when Cat had a cold or was in general need of comforting. A warm baguette, fresh from the oven, scented the kitchen with its fragrant aroma, and Cat knew that her mother was doing everything she could to cheer Cat up. She also knew from the way Poppy was humming that her mother probably felt enormously relieved that Cat hadn't got a place at Ruthersfield. Not that she would ever say such a thing, of course, but Cat could almost feel the relief wafting off her, relief because Cat's future as a witch had come to an abrupt end. Telling her mother she wanted to reapply was not going to be easy.

Every time Cat opened her mouth to say something, the words seemed to jam in her throat. But Marie Claire and her mother didn't seem to notice. They were giving Cat her space, talking quietly to each other.

"I . . . ," Cat began, trying to find her courage. "I . . ."

"Yes, Cat," Poppy said, smiling across the table at her daughter. Cat knew how her mother's face would look when she heard what Cat had to say. She hated upsetting her mother, but Clara Bell was right. She shouldn't give up on her magic just yet. Not if it meant this much to her.

Touching the book in her pocket for good luck, Cat tried again. "Mamma, you and Dad have always encouraged me to follow my dreams, and I wanted this dream more than anything."

"I know you did, sweetheart," Poppy said.

Cat took a sip of water, trying to hold on to her confidence. "I still do, Mamma, and I'd like to reapply again next year." Her voice shook slightly. "There's nothing in the school manual to say I can't."

Poppy glanced at Marie Claire. "Well, let's not think about that now," she answered, sweeping bread crumbs into her hand. "Next year is a long way off."

"Mamma, please," Cat said, wishing her mother

would sound more encouraging. "I saw my friend Clara Bell today. She teaches magical history, and she's a Late Bloomer too. She says there are things I can do to practice getting my magic under control, exercises that can help. And she gave me a book to read, *The Late Bloomer's Guide to Magic*."

"Well, really." Poppy sighed in irritation. "She shouldn't be encouraging you, Cat. That's not fair. Getting your hopes up."

"Mamma." To her distress, Cat felt her lip wobbling.

"Look, you gave it a go. That's what matters." Poppy looked at her daughter with compassion. "I'm proud of you for trying. Now, you have to accept Ms. Roach's decision and move on. I know it's hard, but you don't have a choice."

"Dad would want me to reapply."

Poppy pushed back her chair and stood up. "I'm going to have a little more soup. Cat, you're tired and disappointed, and the supper table is not the place to have this discussion."

"Then when can we have it?" Cat asked. "Because this is important to me."

"I don't know, Cat, sometime. Just not now, all right?" Poppy picked up her bowl and walked over to the stove, bringing the conversation to an end.

The rest of the meal took place in silence, and after

helping with the dishes, Cat went straight upstairs to her room. She hid the bottle of dragon's breath in her sock drawer and then lay down on her bed with *The Late Bloomer's Guide to Magic*. The cover was a pale, faded green, and Cat traced her finger over the faint gold letters. With a feeling of anticipation, she opened the book up to the first page. At the top in purple ink it said, "A few words from Francesca Fenwick." Cat snuggled under her comforter and started to read. "Congratulations on being a Late Bloomer! Inside this book I shall give you tips on controlling your magic, strengthening your core power, and becoming the witch you know you can be. But remember, it is important to spend time around other witches, to watch them perform, to take notes. A good witch can teach you more than any book can."

Oh, if only her mother would help her, Cat thought wistfully, looking up from the page. She must know so much about magic. Cat stared into space for a few moments before focusing back on Francesca Fenwick. "It takes courage and perseverance to succeed as a Late Bloomer, but with the right practice and the right frame of mind, you can have a successful career in magic. Believe in yourself and remember what the great rebel witch, Annabelle Lewis, said when she took down the powers of darkness: Nem zentar topello! — Don't let fear stand in your way!"

"I'll try not to," Cat whispered, cuddling the stuffed lion her dad had brought her back from Africa when she was little. She switched on her bedside lamp for more light and turned to chapter 2, "Adrenaline-Fueled Magic and How to Control It." This was exactly what she needed to know, and Cat gave a little shiver of excitement. "Late bloomer magic can occasionally be triggered by an adrenaline rush," she read. "Fear is the most common catalyst, and this sort of magic can be a challenge to get under control." *Yes it can,* Cat agreed. *Extremely challenging.*

"There are mind exercises to practice in chapter six, but the best way to control fear-triggered magic is to overcome fear itself. Once magic has been activated this way, it will always be unpredictable until you are able to tame your fears. A good witch must stay calm in the face of adversity. She cannot let her fears spiral out of control, because her magic will always suffer. Instead, she must desensitize herself to what frightens her. Face those fears head on so they no longer have the power to scare. Only then will her magic behave."

"So if I overcome my fear of spiders," Cat said, speaking to her stuffed lion, "which is my biggest fear, then I can learn to control my magic. And when I apply to Ruthersfield next year, Ms. Roach will be completely amazed!"

Cat was so encouraged by her plan that she had to tell someone, but since her mother wouldn't understand and she didn't know how to reach Ms. Bell, Cat picked up the walkie-talkie to call Peter. When he didn't respond, Cat decided to go downstairs for a cupcake and a glass of milk. As she passed by the bathroom, Cat could hear water running. Marie Claire took a bath every evening, and Cat wished she had some Amazing Dreams Bath Powder to give her so she could sprinkle a bit in. There were simple instructions on how to make up a batch at the back of *The Late Bloomer's Guide*, but the ingredients called for moon dust, which, Cat knew, was not something they had hanging around the cottage.

Poppy never went to bed this early, and sure enough Cat found her mother in the kitchen, dipping shortbread cookies into melted chocolate. There were two racks of macaroons cooling and a mountain of cookies waiting to be dipped.

"You've been busy," Cat said, taking in her mother's messy braid and the splotches of chocolate and butter on her shirt. She always went into one of her baking marathons when she was feeling stressed.

"I've run out of butter!" Poppy said with a tired

smile. "How am I ever going to sell all of these?"

"You will, Mamma. Everyone loves your baking." Cat picked up a cookie and bit into it. "Oh, if I could only do magic like you bake, I'd be so happy," she said impulsively. Her mother didn't answer. "Mamma, please, will you help me?" Cat begged. "You could teach me so much, and I know if I practice, I'll be good enough to reapply next year."

Poppy thrust down the cookie she was dipping, breaking it in half. "Ms. Roach isn't going to change her mind, Cat. Besides, I'm not allowed to help you with your magic."

"But you could if you wanted. You could show me breathing techniques and simple spells and things."

"Cat, the police could arrest me if they knew I was practicing magic. Look." Poppy was breathing hard. "If you had been offered a place at Ruthersfield, I would have had to accept it, okay. And because I love you, I would have. But it's over. Forget about being a witch." Poppy shook back her braid in frustration. "I wish you had never inherited the stupid gene. All it does is make people miserable. It made me miserable, and now it's doing it's best to ruin your life. Gosh, I hate magic," she fumed as her feet started lifting off the ground. Sometimes, when Poppy's emotions were particularly strong, magic still happened to her. It was not anything

Cat's mother could control or liked, and she gripped the table hard, forcing herself to stay down.

"I thought we talked about things in this family," Cat said. "I thought we had discussions and listened to each other, but you're not listening to me at all."

"Go to bed, Cat. It's late."

"You're doing what you love, Mamma," Cat said with feeling as she walked toward the door. "I just want to do what I love."

Lying in the dark, Cat reached for the walkie-talkie. "Peter, come in," she whispered. "Can you hear me, Peter?" There was no answer. "Peter Parker, are you there?"

"It's ten o'clock," Peter said, his voice sounding thick and slurred.

"I have something important to tell you."

"And it couldn't wait till the morning?"

"No," Cat said firmly, "it couldn't. I've decided to reapply to Ruthersfield next year."

"What! Are you crazy?" There was a rustling of sheets, and for the next ten minutes Cat told him all about her meeting with Clara Bell and *The Late Bloomer's Guide to Magic*, and learning to control her magic by overcoming her fears.

"So if you find any spiders, Peter, please bring

them to school in a match box. That way I can start to get used to them. 'Desensitizing myself,' that's what Francesca Fenwick calls it."

"Can I go to sleep now, Cat? Because you have clearly lost your mind."

"Yes, but please don't forget the spiders."

Chapter Thirteen

···

Disturbing News

CAT KNEW SOMETHING WAS WRONG BEFORE SHE EVEN got downstairs. There was no smell of baking wafting through the cottage. Usually at this time her mother and Marie Claire were already bustling about, filling the bakery shelves with loaves of warm bread and buttery croissants. But this morning nothing was ready. Peeking into the shop, Cat saw that the blinds were still drawn and the glass cases sat empty. What on earth had happened? A nervous feeling gripped Cat's stomach. Maybe Marie Claire had fallen in the night and her mother had taken her to the hospital. Or maybe something awful had happened to her mother?

The bakery was never like this in the mornings, except on Sundays and holidays. The feeling in Cat's stomach got worse. She raced through to the kitchen. "Mamma, where are you?"

Poppy and Marie Claire looked up from the table, a newspaper spread out between them. The radio was on, and the serious voice of a news announcer invaded the kitchen. Mamma and Marie Claire never listened to the news in the morning. There was always music playing.

"What's happened?" Cat said, relieved to see that her mother and Marie Claire were all right.

"A witch has escaped from Scrubs Prison," Poppy said, her voice soft and serious.

"What witch?" Cat asked. "You're scaring me." She sat down at the table, forgetting all about going to school, and pulled the newspaper toward her. "Madeline Reynolds!" Cat cried out, covering her mouth with her hands. "Oh, flipping fish cakes, it's Madeline Reynolds!"

"Now, don't go working yourself into a dither," Poppy said. "Scrubs is a long way from here, Cat." There were two grainy photographs on the front page of the paper. One was of a little girl about Cat's age, dressed in the Ruthersfield uniform. She was smiling at the camera. Underneath was written, "Madeline

Reynolds, age eleven." The other picture showed a bald-headed old woman wearing a boilersuit with the number ten stamped on the front. Her eyes were wild and staring, and Cat glanced from one photo to the other, trying to connect the two. The large, bold headline read, MADELINE REYNOLDS, THE WORLD'S MOST EVIL WITCH, ESCAPES FROM SCRUBS PRISON.

"It is a little bit shocking," Marie Claire said, keeping her voice calm. "Because such a thing has never happened before."

Cat spoke through her hands. "A little bit shocking! She washed away the whole bottom half of Italy."

"*Mon Dieu*, Cat!" Marie Claire said. "Let's not go stirring up the past. That happened a long time ago. She was caught right away and put straight into Scrubs, and I'm sure she'll be back there again very soon."

"I can't believe this!" Cat said, knowing she sounded hysterical. "My worst nightmare has come true."

Poppy stared at the newspaper. "I always thought Madeline Reynolds was sad."

"Sad? She was evil, Mamma."

"No, not 'I've had a bad day' kind of sadness. I mean deeply, painfully sad. The sort of sad that breaks your heart in two and makes you do awful things."

"You sound as if you know her," Cat said. Her mother was making her uncomfortable.

"In a strange way I've always felt like I do," Poppy confessed. "Like we had some kind of connection."

"That is not something I want to hear about, Mamma. I'll start having Madeline Reynolds nightmares again."

"I remember studying her for my biography project. She really loved music. She was this amazing spell chanter," Poppy said, tapping the photograph of the little girl. "Doesn't she look sad to you?"

Cat glanced at the photograph. There was definitely a wistfulness in the little girl's eyes, even though she was smiling.

"I always thought," Poppy added, "that she didn't want to be a witch. That her parents forced her to go to Ruthersfield, like me."

"Even if that's true, it doesn't give her the right to wash away half of Italy," Cat said, wondering how her mother could feel anything but revulsion for this awful creature. "And I don't believe being sad could make someone do something that dreadful," Cat said. "That's just an excuse. She's evil."

Poppy stood abruptly and walked over to the sink. She leaned against it, staring out the window. "Turn the radio up," she said. "I want to listen."

Cat hurried over and twisted the volume on the large red radio that sat on the shelf next to the flour.

"And now," the broadcaster said, "we go direct to

Scrubs Prison to hear from Jeremy Finkle, the guard responsible for Madeline Reynolds's escape."

Marie Claire folded the newspaper up and tucked it under the teapot. Poppy gripped the edge of the sink hard, and Cat stood still, chewing the inside of her lip.

"I'd just taken Madeline her dinner, as usual," Jeremy Finkle said, choking down a sob. "Porridge and grapefruit like she always gets." He paused for a moment, the radio falling silent.

"And then what happened?" the interviewer asked.

"Well, I wasn't wearing my protective glasses," Jeremy Finkle said. "We all have to wear them so we don't look the witches in the eye, you see. They are so full of evil, those witches, and Madeline in particular. Just terrifying." Cat was certain she could hear Jeremy Finkle swallow. "But yesterday evening, well, I couldn't find my glasses and I figured, I've done this a thousand times. I know what I'm doing. I just wouldn't look at her." There was another long silence on the radio.

"And what happened then?" the interviewer prodded.

"I couldn't help myself. She called my name. And before I knew what I was doing, I'd looked right at her. Right into those vile, terrifying eyes." Jeremy Finkle sounded like he was crying. "Somehow she managed to hypnotize me, put me under some sort of spell. I remember this voice in my head, telling me to open the door of her cage. And I did it," Jeremy sobbed. "I let her go. She jumped onto one of the work brooms that we clean the sheds out with and took off, just like that."

"And now a few words from Boris Regal," the interviewer said solemnly. "Head guard at Scrubs Prison."

"She does not have a wand with her, let me make that quite clear," an official-sounding voice said. "Or a proper broomstick. As head guard of Scrubs Prison, I want to assure people not to panic. Well, don't panic too much just yet. Madeline Reynolds is an extremely old witch. We are not underplaying the danger she presents, but she hasn't practiced magic in sixty-five years, although magic was clearly involved in her escape," he admitted. "This matter is being looked into thoroughly, and we feel quite sure she will be captured and brought back to Scrubs very soon."

"Is it true that the top part of Italy has already been evacuated?" the interviewer asked.

"There does seem to be reason to believe that this is where Madeline Reynolds is likely to head, so an evacuation is under way."

"Turn that off, Cat," Marie Claire gasped. "I've heard quite enough."

"Me too," Cat said, wondering what her mother was thinking. Poppy hadn't moved from the sink.

"You should get to school," Marie Claire said. "Sitting here worrying won't help matters."

"Mamma, are you okay?" Cat asked, wishing her mother would turn around.

"Go on now, hurry," Marie Claire said, making shooing motions with her hands. "You are already going to be late."

News of Madeline Reynolds's escape was all over Potts Bottom Elementary by the time Cat got there. She could hear kids whispering about it in class. Cat noticed a number of them giving her funny looks, glancing over quickly and away again, as if she had something to do with it. Concentrating in math was impossible, but when Cat tried to send Peter a note, Ms. Finley, their teacher, crumpled it up and tossed it into the bin before Peter had even read it. Cat had to wait until recess before they could talk.

"That's what the emergency was last night," Peter told her as they stood in the corridor. "All the police stations were informed, and since Ruthersfield is in Potts Bottom and Madeline Reynolds went to school here, my dad's been getting lots of calls."

"I feel sick to my stomach," Cat said. "I wish you

hadn't told me that." She could see Anika and Karen walking toward them. They had their arms linked, and Karen pulled Anika over to the other side of her as they passed by Peter and Cat.

"Her mum used to be just like Madeline Reynolds," Karen whispered loudly.

"You know nothing about my mother," Cat said.

Anika gave Cat a shy smile and tried to pull away from Karen as if she didn't really agree with her.

"I know she runs the bakery and seems as nice as pie," Karen said. "But I still can't believe she went over to the dark side when she was our age."

"Are you talking about Madeline Reynolds?" Emily Willis said, running up to Karen and Anika. She pushed in between them. "Aren't you pleased you don't live in Italy? You know Madeline Reynolds is going to go back there and wash the rest of the country away."

"How do you know that?" Peter asked, rubbing his glasses clean on his shirt.

"Well, that's what everyone says," Emily whispered. "But I'm not at all worried. Nor are my parents. The guards will catch her."

"Come on," Peter said, pulling Cat down the corridor. "Those girls are so stupid. They don't know what they're talking about."

"But the guards will catch her, right?" Cat said, needing to feel reassured. "No wand or broomstick. How dangerous can she be?"

"Look, my dad is really concerned," Peter whispered. "I mean, think about it, Cat. She managed to escape from Scrubs Prison, and no one escapes from Scrubs, do they?"

"Peter, stop it!" Cat covered her ears.

"I thought you were over Madeline Reynolds."

"Well, I lied."

"Wow, you do need to work on your fears!" Peter said. He handed Cat a little Tupperware box. "As you requested! One giant hairy spider that I found in the basement this morning."

Cat could see the spider through the clear plastic container. It looked about the size of a grape, with fat bent legs covered in fur. She shoved it back at Peter with a muffled cry. "I cannot have that in my backpack all day."

"It's not going to hurt you, Cat," Peter said with a grin.

"No!"

"But you asked me to find you one. I even put in a couple of tiny insect things for it to eat."

"I'll collect it after school," Cat said, thinking that conquering this fear of spiders was not going to be as easy as she'd thought. Something tickled the back of her neck and Cat screamed. She reached behind her and slapped Peter's hand away. "That's not funny, Peter," Cat fumed as he cracked up laughing. "Not funny at all!"

Chapter Fourteen

....

Panic in Potts Bottom

MR. ABBOTT, THE HEADMASTER OF POTTS BOTTOM Elementary, had gathered the whole school together so he could talk to them before dismissal that afternoon.

"Now, I know you have heard the news," Mr. Abbott said, standing on a table at the front of the room. He was a little man and wanted to make sure everyone could see him. "But there is no need to panic." He kept dabbing at his sweaty face with a handkerchief, and Cat thought he looked utterly terrified. "This matter will be taken care of by the guards at Scrubs Prison. They are trained to deal with witches from the dark side, and I have no doubt they will handle this in a swift and timely manner. So no one is to worry." Mr. Abbott bared his teeth at them. It was meant to be a smile, Cat realized, but he looked more like one of Auntie Charlie's snaggletoothed goats. The look was not reassuring.

Cat waited for Peter in the school yard. "All right, I'm ready for the spider," she said as he came striding over. Peter tucked the container into the side pocket of Cat's backpack, and she gave a little shudder. "It better not escape."

"That would be funny! Come on. I'll walk with you some of the way."

"Can we swap backpacks?"

"Nope!" Peter shook his head. "You have to be brave, Cat, remember."

Most days after school Cat loved stopping in front of Ruthersfield so she could watch all the girls taking off on their broomsticks. Usually there were a lot of shrieks and giggles as the students swooped into the air. The more advanced girls liked showing off with elegant turns and dives, while the beginners wobbled about on their broomsticks, making shaky trails across the sky. Today though, it was as if someone had put a silencing spell on the academy. There was no chattering or laughter as the girls spilled out of the building. Those who were flying took off quietly into the air, while the walkers headed home with solemn expressions on their faces. Ms. Roach, the headmistress, talked to a group of worried parents, probably trying to calm their fears, Cat guessed. All the teachers looked grave, even Clara Bell, but when she saw Cat she gave her a small, encouraging wave. Two students stood near Cat and Peter on the curb, waiting to be picked up. They had their hats balanced on their bags and were staring at the cars driving past, searching for their ride.

"Hats on, please," a teacher barked out, marching past in her long purple gown. "Good impressions are essential right now." The girls picked up their pointed hats, gave them a shake to get out the creases, and shoved them onto their heads.

"It's so unfair," one of the girls said, after the teacher had gone by. "Just because Madeline Reynolds went to school here, people think Ruthersfield must be to blame. As if we'll all turn out evil."

"My mum says it's witches like her that give the rest of us a bad name," her friend said.

"I know," the first girl grumbled, tucking in her shirt. "So we've all got to be on our best behavior. Especially since Ms. Roach says there are going to be reporters everywhere, getting the backstory on evil old Reynolds."

"Cat, come on." Peter started to walk away. "I feel weird standing here, listening in on their conversations. We'll probably get arrested for loitering."

Cat reluctantly followed Peter down the street, touching a hand to her head and wondering how it would feel to wear a witch's hat. They walked in silence for a while, each caught up in their own thoughts.

"You know, Mamma did a biography project on Madeline Reynolds when she was at school," Cat said at last. "All about how she loved music and singing. Apparently she was a fantastic spell chanter."

"I wonder why your mum would have picked her," Peter said.

Cat suddenly felt too hot inside her jacket, even though there was a bitter wind blowing. She unzipped her anorak, looking away from Peter. It made her so uneasy, thinking that her mother and Madeline Reynolds had anything in common. "Mamma said Madeline Reynolds reminded her of herself," Cat confessed. "She believes she was terribly sad."

"Wow!" Peter tried to catch Cat's eye, but she refused to look at him.

"Mamma thinks Madeline Reynolds didn't want to be a witch," Cat continued. "Just like she didn't want to be one."

"And that's what sent her over to the dark side?"

"Who knows?" Cat shrugged, shoving her hands in her pockets. She finally met Peter's gaze. "Not that any of that matters now, does it? The point is she's the worst storm brewer in history, and she's flying around out there somewhere." A sheet of newspaper went fluttering across the road, and Cat shivered, zipping her jacket back up again.

As she walked down the canal path toward the bakery, Cat could see the door opening and closing, spilling people and light out into the chilly afternoon. The scent of vanilla and chocolate perfumed the air, and Cat knew Marie Claire had made her famous chocolate butter bread. She usually made it only on Wednesdays, which, Marie Claire said, was a day when bad things seemed to happen and people often needed cheering up. But she was clearly making an exception by baking it a day early. After all, you couldn't get much worse than Madeline Reynolds escaping from Scrubs, Cat decided. The windows of the bakery were all fogged up, but Cat could still see how crowded it was inside. It seemed like everyone in Potts Bottom was in need of some comfort eating, and Poppy and Marie Claire were boxing up cakes and macaroons as fast as they could manage. Cat had a hard time opening the door and jostling her way through the crowd. Seeing that poor Marie Claire looked exhausted, Cat threw down her backpack and put on an apron. "You go and sit," she said at once. "I'll take over."

"You are a good girl, *chérie*." Marie Claire hobbled over to the kitchen door, and Cat noticed how swollen her ankle looked.

"Put your feet up, Marie Claire. When it calms down here, I'll make you a cup of tea."

"I said a loaf of chocolate butter bread and ten cupcakes, please," Mrs. Mitchell shouted at Cat. Mrs. Mitchell was the town librarian and never raised her voice, so this was most unlike her. Cat could feel the anxiety hovering over the villagers.

"It's been like this all day," Poppy whispered, wrapping ribbon around a box of lemon tarts. "Everyone is nervous."

Maxine Gibbons was huddled in a corner of the shop, talking to Mrs. Plunket. She had a loaf of bread clutched in her arms but clearly wasn't ready to leave.

"I mean, it's bringing back all sorts of memories," Maxine said, not even bothering to keep her voice down. Cat had never understood why her grandmother spent so much time at Maxine's house. Glancing at the counter, Maxine nodded at Cat and then turned right back to Mrs. Plunket. Lowering her voice a bit, but still speaking loud enough for Cat to hear, she went on, "Honestly, I'm far too nervous to sleep tonight. I'll never forget when Poppy went over to the dark side. Just like Madeline Reynolds, she was."

"Can I get you anything else, Mrs. Gibbons?" Cat called out sweetly. "We're awfully crowded in here, so if you've finished your shopping, do you mind making room for other people?"

Poppy gave her daughter a grateful smile as Maxine stalked out of the shop. "She's been in here for almost an hour," Poppy murmured.

"Well, it's about time she left then, isn't it?" Cat replied, suddenly feeling protective toward her mother. It was okay for Cat to be mad at her, but it was not okay for Maxine Gibbons to say mean things.

By the time the bakery closed, there was nothing left on the shelves except for a few raspberry shortbread cookies. Cat swept the floor and wiped down the counters, while Poppy locked the front door and emptied the cash register. "Thank you so much for all your help, Cat," Poppy said. "I couldn't have managed without you this afternoon."

"Are you okay, Mamma?" Cat asked. Her mother's face was pale as cake flour, and she had lines etched across her forehead.

"It's bringing back memories for me, as well," Poppy said. "Not just for nosy old Maxine." She tucked a strand of loose hair back into her braid and forced herself to smile. "Anyway, I don't need to be thinking about the past, do I? If tomorrow is anything like today, I'll have to get started on my bread doughs. I've never seen the bakery this busy." She kissed Cat on the forehead as she walked past, an impulsive kiss that made Cat suddenly brave.

"Mamma?" Poppy stopped and turned around. "Could you just watch me practice some spell breathing exercises?" Cat said. "Tell me if I'm doing them right. It's meant to be a good way to help with control."

"Cat, please." Poppy held up her hand. "I can't deal with this right now. Honestly, how can you even think about magic with Madeline Reynolds on the loose?"

"Because I love it." Cat gripped the broom hard. "And I would never end up on the dark side, Mamma. You know that."

Poppy opened the door behind the counter that led to the rest of the cottage. "Well, thank goodness you won't get the chance to find out," she said. "Now no more talk of Ruthersfield, okay?"

Letting the broom clatter to the floor, Cat ran upstairs to her room.

Chapter Fifteen

....

Spiders Are a Girl's Best Friend

*T*HE LATE BLOOMER'S GUIDE TO MAGIC LAY OPEN ON Cat's bed. Since her mother had refused to help her, Cat would just have to do this by herself. There was no other way. If she wanted to learn to control her magic, she had to start conquering her fears.

It took Cat fifteen minutes to open the container with the spider in it. Every time she got close to lifting the lid, she'd cram the top on again and back away. "I can't do it," Cat whispered. "I just can't." What if the spider crawled up her sleeve, scurrying over her skin on its fat furry legs? Spiders moved so fast. One of the things Francesca Fenwick advised in her book was that naming your fears made them easier to face, so Cat decided to call the spider Boris, hoping this might make her feel less scared of him. This was all much harder than she had anticipated, and by the time she finally got the lid off and peeked inside, her palms were damp with sweat and her face was flushed pink. Once she had done it though, it wasn't quite as hard the next time. Cat managed to take the lid on and off twice more before her mother called her down for dinner. On the third time Cat even managed to hold the container in her hand rather than peering into it on the floor.

Dinner was a quiet affair. Over shepherd's pie and peas, Marie Claire did most of the talking while Cat and her mother said very little, avoiding eye contact with each other. It was a relief when the meal finally ended, and after helping wash the dishes, Cat went straight back up to her room. She planned to practice a little bit more. Maybe even touch Boris with a finger, but her skin tingled at the mere thought, and Cat decided she might not be ready for that yet.

"Cat, are you there?" Peter said, his voice crackling through the walkie-talkie.

Cat grabbed the receiver and sat on her bed. "I'm making friends with the spider, Peter. I've called him Boris."

"Cat, listen a second. This is really important." Peter was breathing hard. "I think I've worked out where Madeline Reynolds is going. And it's definitely not Italy!" There was a crackly pause. "You're not going to like this, but I thought you'd want know so you could be prepared. I'm quite certain she's coming here to Potts Bottom."

"What?" Cat hunched up her legs, glancing around her room. "How on earth did you figure that?"

"You have to go back to the root of the problem to find out the answer," Peter said, sounding excited. "Just like a simple math equation."

"I'm not following at all, Peter, and you're making me extremely nervous."

"Well, I've been mulling over what your mum told you. How she always thought Madeline Reynolds was sad because she didn't want to be a witch."

Cat could almost hear Peter jiggling up and down. She imagined his hair sticking out in wild, frizzy clumps the way it always did whenever he had one of his brain waves.

"And I keep looking at that photograph of her in the paper, Cat, and she does look sad."

"But why would that make her come back to Potts Bottom?"

"Because this is where her unhappiness began. At

Ruthersfield," Peter said. "Just like Auntie Poppy." There was a burst of static. "Can you hear me, Cat?"

"I can hear you."

"I bet she's so angry at this place, she's planning to come back here and do something really awful," Peter continued. "Imagine being locked up in jail for years and years, all that evilness and anger brewing away. And then you escape. You bust free. Who would you want to take your fury out on?"

"Peter, stop it!" Cat cried out at the same time that Peter yelled, "Ruthersfield!"

"Now I'm not going to sleep one wink tonight. Have you told your dad?"

"Course I have," Peter answered. "He yawned, said 'Nice idea, Pete, reminds me of your asteroid one!' and flopped onto the sofa. Apparently every police precinct in the country—actually in the whole world—has been flooded with calls from people worrying that Madeline Reynolds is coming to their town."

"Well, I really wish you hadn't told me."

"But it makes such perfect sense," Peter said proudly. "I'm sure I'm right."

"Which is why I wish you hadn't told me," Cat snapped, switching off her walkie-talkie.

Suddenly Boris didn't seem quite so scary. Cat put his container on her bedside table and picked up the old cardboard periscope. She dangled it over the side of her bed and looked through the top, which from Peter's clever angling of mirrors showed her exactly what was going on underneath. To Cat's great relief, apart from a great many dust balls, there was no Madeline Reynolds hiding there. She wished she could call downstairs for reassurance. When Cat had been little, Poppy used to climb onto her bed and cuddle her fears away. There was nothing more comforting than the solid warmth and cake smell of her mother. But that certainly wasn't going to happen tonight.

A dog barked outside, and goose bumps broke out on Cat's arms. Fear shot up her spine, and she scurried over to shut the curtains. Usually Cat liked seeing the moon above the canal, the same moon that her dad was looking at somewhere on the other side of the world. It made Cat feel closer to him, but tonight with Madeline Reynolds on the loose, she drew her curtains tight.

If Cat slept at all, it was only very lightly, dozing off somewhere around five a.m. She had spent the night with her lights on and the wand under her pillow for protection. Not that she would ever get her magic under control with fear welling up inside her like rising bread dough. Spiders she could manage. It was this big, smothering panic that threatened to overwhelm her every time she thought about Madeline Reynolds.

That was the fear she needed to conquer. There was no way Cat's magic would behave until she could manage this. "And that will never happen," Cat said, realizing she was talking to Boris. He looked almost friendly this morning, and a small beam of pride glowed inside her. A few days ago Cat would never have imagined making friends with a spider. But if she could master spiders, maybe, just maybe, she could master Madeline Reynolds. After all, Cat tried to convince herself, the real Madeline Reynolds couldn't possibly be as awful as the witch Cat imagined in her head, could she? And besides, it was just too tiring, being this frightened of a childhood terror. She had to start getting some sleep. "Don't let fear stand in your way," Clara Bell had said. And she was right. If Cat wanted to go to Ruthersfield and be a witch and do what she knew she was destined to do, she couldn't let Madeline Reynolds stop her.

"Boris, I believe I'm getting an idea," Cat whispered to the spider. "It's what my dad would call a 'wild idea,' but I think it just might work." She considered waking Peter up to tell him about it, but Peter was not a morning person. And since Cat didn't feel like getting shouted at right now, she decided to wait until she saw him at school.

Chapter Sixteen

....

A Sticky Situation

I'VE HAD AN IDEA," CAT TOLD PETER LATER THAT MORN-
ing, waylaying him on his way to science club. "I
think you're right about Madeline Reynolds coming
back here."

"I know," Peter nodded. "Adam says I'm brilliant.
No one else seems to believe me," he added.

"Well, I do, and I'm going to try to capture her," Cat
said, keeping her voice soft.

"What? Oh, you're joking!" Peter laughed. "For a
second there I thought you were serious."

"I am serious," Cat said, gripping Peter's arm. "It
makes perfect sense."

"It makes no sense whatsoever. You're terrified of Madeline Reynolds."

"I was terrified of spiders until yesterday, and now Boris and I are rather good friends. In fact, I'm thinking of keeping him as a pet."

"Boris?"

"My spider. Well, your spider. But the point is I'm not that frightened of him anymore."

"Cat, you cannot compare a spider to Madeline Reynolds. A spider wouldn't hurt a fly—well maybe a fly—but spiders are soft and hairy and good for the environment, and Madeline Reynolds washed away half of Italy."

"She's also eighty-five years old and she doesn't have a broomstick or a wand with her. Look," Cat said impatiently. "If I can conquer my fear of Madeline Reynolds, I'll definitely be able to get my magic under control, and think about what Ms. Roach would say." Cat gave an excited little jump. "She'd see how dedicated to magic I am. How brave I can be. She'd have to give me a place. I'll probably get fast-tracked to broomstick flying right away."

"Small question," Peter said, "but quite an important one. How do you propose to do this?"

"Well, no one except for me, you, and Adam believes that she's coming here, so I'm not going to have any competition from the police or anything. I just need to find a good spell."

"I've said this already, but I'm going to say it again. You're terrified of Madeline Reynolds."

"That's why I have to do this," Cat explained. "Francesca Fenwick says naming your fears takes away some of the power they have over you, but since Madeline Reynolds already has a name, I thought I'd give her a nickname. Like Maddie. That's much less scary, isn't it?"

"The worrying thing is you actually think this is a good idea," Peter said.

"I thought you might like to come home after school with me today so I could practice on you."

"Absolutely, one hundred percent no way."

"Oh, Peter, please. I think you'll find I'm getting better."

"You are not practicing magic on me, Cat. I have seen your magic, don't forget."

"Then I'll practice on Boris, which will probably be better anyway, because I'm still a bit scared of him. He'll be good training for Maddie."

"Cat, you are bat flaking nuts," Peter said. "Just take your walkie-talkie with you, okay? Because I guarantee you're going to need to call for help."

"Thanks for your support," Cat said rather huffily.

"Just being honest," Peter replied with a shrug, heading off to science club.

It would probably be best not to practice magic in the bakery, Cat decided, just in case things didn't go as planned. Not that she expected anything to go wrong, but it was good to be prepared. Cat grabbed the copy of *Practical Magic* from the box under her bed and shoved it into a bag, along with Boris's container and the wand. At the last minute she slipped the walkie-talkie in too, wrapping a few more rubber bands around the booster box to keep it in place. Marie Claire and her mother were busy in the shop, so Cat slipped out through the kitchen door and headed for the little shed that her dad had built. It housed the lawn mower, some old paint cans, and a collection of assorted junk, and was, Cat decided, the perfect place for practicing magic.

She sat down on a sack of organic fertilizer and started to flip through *Practical Magic*. Clearly her mother had used this volume a lot, because a number of the pages were stuck together and covered in sticky stains. "The Stop It Now Spell might work," Cat murmured. It was supposed to freeze fast-moving objects, but what if Madeline Reynolds wasn't fast moving? What if she just stood there flinging magic around? On page ninety-two Cat found something even better. The Trapped like a Fly Spell looked perfect. Running her finger down the page, Cat read, "The Trapped like a Fly Spell has many uses. It is mainly performed as a way of restraining out of control individuals. Highly effective when used to truss up a child in the middle of a tantrum, keeping them safe and out of danger until the tantrum has passed. A convenient carrying loop is attached to the back of the binding."

Long sticky threads were meant to shoot out of your wand, "tying up your target like a spider wrapping up a fly," Cat read.

"Except you're going to be the one getting wrapped up," she told Boris, lifting his container out of the bag.

"So wave the wand in a smooth spinning spiral," Cat murmured, "and in a loud, clear voice say, 'Intra . . .'"

She frowned and studied the word. It was a hard one to pronounce. "'Intra . . . Intratangledcat.' No, that's not right." Cat sighed and tried again, saying the word slowly as she ran her finger underneath it. "'Intratangledcacoono!' Yes!" She fist-punched the air and practiced a few more times to make sure she had got it correct.

"Well, that all looks okay," Cat said, speaking to her spider. "Now I'm going to open the lid and let you out, Boris. But please don't do that scuttling thing, all right?" She could feel her heart starting to race as she flipped off the lid. He looked so fat and hairy, and Cat took a couple of deep breaths to calm herself. "Ready, Boris?" She tipped the container over and scrambled to her feet.

Holding the wand tight, Cat pointed it at the spider and made a rather jerky spiraling motion. "Intratangledcacoono!" she said in a clear, confident voice, just as Boris scurried toward her as if he was racing to see an old friend. Cat screamed, falling backward over the sack of fertilizer.

Her spell bounced off the ceiling and ricocheted straight down, wrapping her up in a tangle of sticky threads. The fact that she couldn't really move and had no idea where Boris had gone made Cat scream again.

Wiggling her hand, she managed to grab the walkie-talkie. Cat could push the button, but she couldn't hold the receiver to her mouth because her arms were trapped. "Peter," Cat yelled. "Can you hear me?" *Please be in your room. Please be there,* Cat prayed.

"Problem?" Peter replied as if he had been waiting for her to call.

"Please come to the garden shed, right now. And bring a pair of scissors."

✸ ✸ ✸ ✸

"I'm not going to say 'I told you, Cat,' but I did tell you," Peter said, attempting to cut her free. It wasn't easy because the threads kept sticking to the scissors. "This is an absolute mess. Not a tidy, neat bundle like the book says. And where's your carrying loop?"

"Look, it may not be perfect, but the spell worked," Cat pointed out. "It didn't go crazy and dance out of the shed. I fell over, which was my fault, and it bounced back on me, but it still worked." She felt rather pleased with herself, especially since Peter had found Boris and put him safely back in his container. "I was hoping you might make me a Madeline Reynolds detector," Cat asked him. "So I'll know when she gets here."

"You won't need one," Peter snapped. "She's a storm brewer, Cat. Just look for a big change in the weather." He wiped white, sticky goo off his glasses and said, "I think you're taking this magic thing too far. Trying to catch Madeline Reynolds is ridiculous. You can't even catch a spider. I bet you don't have a backup plan, do you?"

"No, but we could think of one together," Cat suggested. "Just in case."

"There is no 'we' involved here," Peter said. "I think you're crazy. I think this whole idea is crazy. Madeline Reynolds is the worst storm brewer in history. You really want to go to Ruthersfield so badly, you're going to risk your life?"

"Yes," Cat whispered, wishing Peter wouldn't sound so mad. "My dad says you risk your life every time you walk out your front door, Peter. I'm not giving up yet."

....

Chapter Seventeen

A Cake to Raise Your Spirits

THE FOLLOWING MORNING AS CAT WALKED INTO THE kitchen, she was greeted by the low, monotonous voice of the radio broadcaster. "Still no news of Madeline Reynolds's whereabouts," he said. Her mother and Marie Claire were rolling out croissant dough in silence. "Italy has now been completely evacuated," the presenter continued. "Highly trained guards are positioned and waiting for what is expected to be the imminent arrival of Madeline Reynolds."

"Oh, please!" Marie Claire said, limping over to the radio and turning it off. "Honestly, I've heard enough. Do people have nothing else to talk about? All this hysteria over an old woman. She has no wand and she's been locked in a cage most of her life. What on earth can she possibly do?"

"I quite agree, Marie Claire," Cat said with enthusiasm.

"You can't imagine what it feels like," Poppy burst out, sprinkling raisins over the dough, "being full of hatred and darkness." Cat had never seen her mother look so unwell. She had dark shadows under her eyes, and Cat guessed she had slept in her braid. "I do. I've been there, and it doesn't matter how old you are. You can still do terrible things. I was ten years old and I turned my parents to stone." Cat flinched at the strength of her mother's words.

"With good reason," Marie Claire murmured. "You were not to blame, Poppy."

"It doesn't matter. I did it. And no one has any idea what Madeline Reynolds is capable of doing."

Cat's stomach flipped over. She wished her mother hadn't said that.

A gentle thud sounded from the bakery. "Was that the postman?" Poppy jerked her head up, glancing toward the shop. He usually came early, before Cat left for school, dropping the mail through their brass letter slot so it landed in a heap on the floor.

"I'll go and look," Cat offered, hoping that there

might be some word from her father. It had been so long since a letter had come from him. She knew her mother was hoping for the same thing, because as Cat left the room she heard her say to Marie Claire, "It's not just Madeline Reynolds, you know. I'm worried about Tristram, too." Cat stopped to listen. She couldn't help herself. Her mother never worried about her father in front of Cat, but she obviously felt just as anxious. "It's been weeks since we heard any news. I know he can't call because there's no service where he is, but he's always managed to send letters before."

A weak, sick feeling clutched Cat. What if something had happened to her dad? But she couldn't think that way. "You've got to believe, Cat." That's what her dad always told her, never saying what it was he believed in exactly. Just that if you did believe, it would most certainly all be all right. And so far he had not been proved wrong, returning from the jungles of Africa, where he had almost been eaten by lions, searching for the big-leafed bilibead plant, and the mountains of Nepal, where he spent three weeks trapped in an underground tunnel living on nothing but worms and water. And now, even though no one had heard from Tristram Campbell in two months, Cat still forced herself to believe that he would be fine. But there were no postcards with foreign stamps on them written in her dad's scrawling hand, and when Cat brought the mail through, she couldn't hide the disappointment on her face.

"Cat?" Marie Claire said, rolling a triangle of dough into a croissant. "Can you put on some nice music, *chérie*? We all need a little cheering up around here, I think. Something to lift our spirits."

"Lift our spirits," Cat mused, walking over to the radio. As she fiddled with the buttons, tuning it in to the classical music station Marie Claire loved, a slow smile spread across her face. "I know this is going to surprise you both, but I'd like to make a cake this afternoon," Cat said, thinking that maybe it wasn't just music they needed to cheer them all up. "Something easy and delicious to make us feel better."

"What a lovely idea," Marie Claire said.

Even Poppy smiled. "There's nothing like baking to help you forget your worries," she agreed.

Cat slipped Boris's container into her backpack, deciding to take him to school. She had to keep working on desensitizing herself, although Boris seemed to be her only friend at the moment anyway. Most of the kids wouldn't go near her, and all everyone talked about was Madeline Reynolds. Even Peter didn't sit with Cat at lunch, so she propped Boris's container on the table to keep her company, wishing she had access to some unicorn milk. There was a simple recipe for a Friendship Repair Hot Chocolate at the back of *The Late Bloomer's Guide*, and Cat would have loved to make some for Peter. Or if she had a jar of pixie laughs handy, she could have whipped up a batch of Shortbread Giggle Bars to get him laughing again. Cat could tell he was still annoyed with her, because he wouldn't even look in her direction, and on his way out of the cafeteria with Adam, he marched over and said, "I'm hoping you've changed your mind, Cat."

"I haven't." Cat shook her head. "I'm going to try to let Boris crawl on me tonight. If I shut my eyes, I think I'll be able to do it. Then I can practice the spell again. See if I'm improving."

"Your mum would be so mad if she knew what you were planning," Peter hissed, and stuffing his hands in his pockets, he stalked off after Adam.

Cat wasn't too sure how her mother would feel if she knew the sort of cake Cat intended to bake either. But there was so much gloominess in the bakery at the moment, it would be nice to cheer her mother and Marie Claire up. And once Poppy tasted it, Cat reasoned, she would be in such a good mood that maybe they could have a proper discussion about Cat reapplying to Ruthersfield. And perhaps, Cat thought hopefully (it was a wild hope, she knew), her mother might even be a little bit proud of Cat for mastering a proper spell. "Although I haven't mastered it yet," Cat told herself, assembling ingredients on the kitchen table as soon as she got home from school.

Earlier she had flipped through her mother's old copy of *The Compendium of Witchcraft Cookery* to see what a complicated cooking spell looked like. There was an advanced recipe in it for a Raising Your Spirits Cake, but it was meant for "extremely sad people" and called for things like two cups of self-rising west wind flour, three phoenix eggs, and a dash of butterfly dreams — ingredients Cat hadn't even heard of. She knew she would have to start with something far simpler.

Her mother and Marie Claire were both busy in the bakery, so there was no one to disturb Cat as she worked. Being careful not to spill anything on *The Late Bloomer's Guide to Magic*, Cat mixed sugar and butter in a large bowl and cracked in two eggs. She sifted flour on top, poured in a little milk, and then carefully unscrewed the top of the purple bottle Ms. Bell had given her. "One teaspoon of condensed dragon's breath," Cat whispered, glancing at the recipe. She tipped the bottle over a measuring spoon and a smoldering red cloud puffed out. It filled the bowl of the spoon, streams of smoke drifting into the air. Cat poured the dragon's breath onto the batter. She watched it float down, evaporating into a red mist as it touched the cake mixture. "'Hold a wooden (not metal) spoon in your left hand,'" Cat read out loud. "'Making sure you start in a clockwise direction, begin stirring the batter, and in a clear, cheerful voice, chant the following spell.

> Sunshine, moonbeams, light as air
> Stir three times round without a care.
> Warm winds, laughter, spirits rise
> Stir back three times, counterclockwise.'"

Cat stopped halfway through stirring and began again, realizing she had started out counterclockwise, not clockwise. The batter was a pale pink color, and Cat tingled with excitement as she scraped the mixture into a tin and popped it in the oven.

It was as she cleaned up her mess that she realized she had used the tablespoon measure for the dragon's breath and not the teaspoon. *Well, it's too late to worry about that now,* Cat reasoned. Her cake would just make everyone extra cheerful.

"Something smells delicious!" Marie Claire said, limping into the kitchen. She stared at the odd-looking pink cake sitting on the table. "My goodness, *chérie*! You really did bake a cake! Your mother will be so proud."

"I hope so," Cat said, cutting Marie Claire a fat slice. "You can have the first piece, Marie Claire."

Marie Claire closed her eyes and took a bite. "Vanilla, and something else I can't quite put my finger on. Mmmm." She smiled in contentment. "It's delicious."

"I thought it might cheer you and Mamma up," Cat said. "You've both been working so hard."

"Oh!" Marie Claire started to laugh. "Oh, my goodness." She giggled as her feet lifted off the ground. "Whatever did you put in here, Cat? I'm floating!"

"Flipping fish cakes!" Cat whispered, watching Marie Claire continue to rise and drift over toward the oven.

"What a wonderful feeling!" Marie Claire sighed, leaning back on the air and kicking her legs up. She grasped her hands behind her neck. "I'm so happy, Cat. I feel light as a feather and free as a bird." She started laughing again, as if this was the funniest thing that had ever happened to her.

"Marie Claire, I'm so sorry," Cat said, panicking. "This is all my fault. It was meant to be a simple Raising Your Spirits Cake, but I obviously got the spell a bit wrong."

"My spirits have never been better, Cat. But you

should probably take me into my bedroom before your mother discovers what has happened."

"Oh, please, don't tell her," Cat whispered, reaching up to give Marie Claire a gentle push into the hallway. Luckily the door to the bakery was shut, so Poppy couldn't see Cat nudge a floating Marie Claire up the stairs. "Mamma would be so mad if she knew what I've done."

"Then I'd get rid of the rest of that cake pretty quickly," Marie Claire said, laughing, as she wafted into her bedroom. "Before your mother has a slice!"

Leaving Marie Claire hovering above her bed, Cat raced back downstairs, and while Poppy finished closing up the shop, she chucked the remains of the cake outside. "I put too much salt in it," Cat told her mother when Poppy finally appeared in the kitchen.

"But how nice you're taking an interest in baking," Poppy replied, plopping down in a chair and rubbing her feet. "Gosh, it's been like a zoo out there all day. I'm exhausted."

"So is Marie Claire," Cat said quickly, not meeting her mother's gaze. "She's having a little rest. I said I'd take her up some soup later on."

Marie Claire was still floating at dinnertime, but only an inch or two above her bed. She had managed to slide under the covers, which helped weigh her down a little bit, and was singing away happily in French.

"I cannot imagine what Marie Claire is so happy about," Poppy said as she washed up the dishes after supper.

Cat shrugged and continued clearing the table, trying to hide her guilt.

"I didn't sleep at all last night," Poppy confessed, resting her hands on the sink. She frowned and leaned forward, staring hard through the window. "What in the . . ." Poppy began, rubbing at her eyes. "That can't be. It's just not possible."

Hurrying over, Cat peered through the glass to see what her mother was looking at. By the light of the moon she could just make out a handful of chickens floating around the yard, wafting gently on the breeze like helium balloons. No wonder her mother looked so shocked!

Bending over the sink, Poppy splashed cold water on her face. She patted it dry with a towel and walked rather shakily across the room. "I'm going to bed," Poppy murmured, rubbing her eyes again. "I'm so tired I'm seeing things."

"Night, Mamma," Cat called after her, praying that the chickens would be back on the ground by tomorrow. She'd have to be more careful with her measuring and stirring next time, but the spell hadn't been a complete failure, Cat decided. The chickens didn't seem to mind, and Marie Claire certainly appeared happier.

Cat knew she should let Boris out for a little crawl on her hand. If she was serious about facing Madeline Reynolds, she needed to be prepared. But the thought of Boris scuttling all over her at this moment just wasn't something she felt up to. That could wait until tomorrow. Smothering a yawn, Cat was about to turn off the lights when she noticed a crumb of pink cake lying on the table, the size of a small pea. She eyed it for a moment, and then, making up her mind, Cat darted over and popped the crumb into her mouth. It was so small she couldn't taste much, just a little sweetness and maybe a hint of vanilla. However, Cat was smiling as she climbed up the stairs. Suddenly everything felt more hopeful.

Chapter Eighteen

....

Mothers Don't Always Know Best

THE NEXT MORNING CAT WAS RELIEVED TO FIND MARIE Claire standing at the kitchen table, rolling out croissants. And even more relieved to see the chickens clucking around the yard as usual.

"I'm feeling extremely light on my feet this morning," Marie Claire said, giving Cat a wink.

Poppy, on the other hand, was hunched over a tray of cupcakes, piping on frosting and reading the newspaper at the same time. "They still don't know where she is," Poppy murmured. "No sign of Madeline Reynolds anywhere."

Cat shuddered. Any day now, the world's most evil

storm brewer could turn up in Potts Bottom, and Cat had to be ready.

When Cat got home from school, the bakery was jammed with customers. She felt a touch guilty as she slipped upstairs to her room, knowing Poppy and Marie Claire could use her help, but she had to keep working on her fears. "Okay, Boris, now I'm going to let you out for a little walk," Cat said. "Please go slowly and don't run up my sleeve." She opened the container and, before she could change her mind, Cat tipped him onto her open palm. "Ohhhhh," she wailed softly, but she didn't flick him off right away. "One, two, three, four, five," Cat said, before giving her hand a violent shake. Boris dropped onto the floor, and Cat gave a sob of relief. "Five seconds — I did it!"

She rubbed her hands together to get rid of the ticklish feeling and pulled *Practical Magic* out from under the bed. Cat had memorized the Trapped like a Fly Spell by heart, but she wanted to read over the wand technique again. "Right, Boris, get ready to be tied up," Cat said.

"Cat, are you in there?" Poppy knocked on her daughter's door. "We could do with a hand."

"I'm studying," Cat called back, slipping her magic wand under the rug.

"Are you all right?" Poppy said, opening the door and stepping inside.

"Mamma, I'm busy." Cat slammed the spell book shut and shoved it behind her.

"Cat! What exactly are you doing?" Poppy walked across the room and plucked the book up before Cat could stop her. She looked at the cover. "*Practical Magic*?"

"I'm just reading it."

"You shouldn't even have this." Poppy gasped, glancing around the room. "You found it in the attic, didn't you?" Her voice rose in anger. "Where are the others, Cat? I'm sure my mother kept them all." Poppy got down on her hands and knees and peered under the bed. She pulled out the box of magic books. "Now I know where you've been getting your spells from."

"Mamma, please."

"I cannot believe you're up here practicing magic," Poppy fumed.

"Don't take them away," Cat begged.

"I most certainly will," Poppy said, holding the box in her arms. "I'm your mother, Cat, and I know what's best for you."

"You think you do, but you don't." Cat couldn't believe what her mother had just done. "You mustn't throw them away."

"I'm not going to throw them away. I just don't want to see you get hurt."

"No, you don't want to see me do magic." Cat started to shake, anger rushing through her in a torrent.

Poppy knelt down on the rug beside her daughter, balancing the box of books in her lap. "This is becoming an obsession, Cat. Ms. Roach isn't going to change her mind. I know what she's like, and you need to find something else to focus on. What about gymnastics or horseback riding? I'd even support you if you wanted to run away and join the circus." Poppy gave a wobbly laugh, but Cat didn't join in.

"Please let me keep the books, Mamma."

Poppy gave a deep sigh and stood up. "I've made a nice chicken pie for supper," she said softly. "You'll feel better after you've had something to eat."

"No, I won't," Cat whispered, realizing that as well as losing her books she had also lost sight of Boris. Her spider was nowhere to be seen. If she had had the power to turn her mother to stone right then, she might have done it.

The weather turned wintry overnight. There was frost on the grass when Cat left for school in the mornings. Ten days had passed since Madeline Reynolds escaped. The villagers took to wearing dark-colored clothing as if all the browns and blacks and stormy purple sweaters reflected their bleak, gloomy mood. Nobody smiled, and the lines outside the bakery wound right along the canal path and up to the street as the villagers lined up in worried silence for their cakes and croissants and warm butter bread. Cat had stopped speaking to her mother, Peter had gone back to sitting with Adam on the bus, and it was difficult for Cat not to feel her own spirits starting to droop. Her dream of becoming a witch seemed to be slipping further and further out of reach.

On Friday afternoon, Cat hurried straight home from school, so caught up in her own thoughts that she didn't notice Clara Bell coming out of the bakery until they almost collided with each other. "Sorry," Cat apologized, looking up. "I didn't see you coming."

"No harm done," Clara Bell said, closing the shop door behind her. "And lucky for me, I just got the last loaf of walnut bread. Beat old Maxine Gibbons to it!"

"That's nice." Cat forced herself to smile. "The shop's never been this busy."

"Comfort eating," Clara Bell said. "I have to admit I bought cookies as well."

"Are you nervous?" Cat asked her. "About Madeline Reynolds being out there somewhere?"

"A touch, I suppose. But I try to save my worrying for things I have some control over." Clara Bell shifted the bags in her arms, rustling the thin white paper. "And how are you doing?" she asked gently, her brown eyes full of warmth. "Did my little book help?"

"It did," Cat said, glancing over at the canal. "Although no one seems to think it's a good idea for me to reapply to Ruthersfield next year." She didn't mention her plan to try to capture Madeline Reynolds, because she knew how crazy it would sound.

"But you still do?"

"I want to, more than anything," Cat said, her lip beginning to quiver.

"Believing in yourself and your magic is half the battle, Cat. That's one of Francesca Fenwick's most helpful tips, I think."

"I'm trying to believe," Cat said, "but it's so hard. I'm beginning to think it's not worth it. I can't do it. I'm making everyone unhappy."

"You have to have a great deal of courage to be a Late Bloomer," Clara Bell said. She slipped a hand into one of the bags and took out a raspberry jam shortbread. "I didn't quite tell you my full story before, Cat, but when I was at college, I took potions class as well as history. That's what I really wanted to be, a potions teacher, but I got an F in my exams."

"An F?"

"I know. I was devastated, but I chose not to retake them because I was scared I'd fail again. And now I'll never know what might have happened."

"I thought you loved teaching magical history," Cat said.

"Oh, I do, I really do," Clara Bell said. "And maybe things would have turned out like this anyway. I just wish I'd been braver back then, that's all." She popped the cookie into her mouth and chewed. "Don't let fear stand in your way, Cat."

When Cat woke on Saturday morning, it was still dark. The quiet buzz of the radio drifted through the floorboards, along with the smell of coffee cupcakes. Cat buried her face in her pillow, hating the sweet scent. It reminded her of happy weekends, making pretend magic potions at the kitchen table while her mother and Marie Claire baked. A great wave of self-pity engulfed her. But feeling sorry for herself wasn't going to solve anything, and Cat picked up *The Late Bloomer's Guide to Magic*. At least her mother hadn't taken this book away, although if she'd seen it sitting on the nightstand, Cat knew she would have. She started reading chapter 7, which was all about the importance of positive attitudes. By the time the postman arrived, Cat's spirits had lifted and she could hear Ted Roberts whistling as she raced downstairs. He gave Cat a big smile as she opened the bakery door and handed her a stack of letters.

"You're in a good mood," Cat said. "I haven't seen anyone this happy in Potts Bottom all week."

"I've stopped worrying, Cat. I decided this morning. I said, 'Ted Roberts, you can't spend the rest of your life worrying about something that may never happen.'" The postman shifted his bag of mail over to his other shoulder. "Besides," he added, "if you ask me, I think she fell off that work broom over the Pacific Ocean and got eaten by a shark."

"I haven't heard that idea before," Cat said.

"No? Well, it makes sense, doesn't it? My mother's the same age as Madeline Reynolds and she has trouble just getting up the stairs. So how's an eighty-five-year-old witch going to go gadding about on a work broom? Tell me that." Ted Roberts nodded at the mail in Cat's hands. "I think you'll find something interesting in there," he said, giving Cat another huge grin.

Cat found the postcard wedged in between the electricity bill and the phone bill. It had a waterfall on the front, and when Cat turned it over, she read:

> *Dear Cat,*
>
> *Congratulations on getting the gift! I know you'll make a wonderful witch!!*
>
> *Love, Dad*
>
> *PS — Tell Mum I love her and I'm on my way home. Found myself in a bit of a sticky situation, but things are all right now.*

This was an omen. It had to be. Cat smiled at the postcard and gave it a kiss. Her dad believed in her. He said so, right there in red pen. She'd make a wonderful witch. And whatever her mother thought, Cat wasn't going to give up on her dream.

Chapter Nineteen

··

A Wave of Low Pressure

THE DAY GOT DARKER AND MORE OMINOUS AS IT WORE on, and Cat began to wonder if she believed in good omens. She spent most of her time helping out in the bakery, dealing with rude customers who were too anxious to be polite. The mood in Potts Bottom had hit an all time low. Poor Marie Claire's ankle was hurting so badly she couldn't stand for long, so Cat and her mother worked side by side in silence. Even the news that Cat's dad was coming home couldn't thaw the ice between them.

As soon as the bakery closed, Cat grabbed the last two lemon bars and went straight to her room, but the minute she shut the door, she wished she had gone for a walk instead. She had been stuck in the bakery all day, and her bedroom felt too small and stuffy. Cat paced around a few times and finally yanked open her window. Sometimes, on nice days or when the moon was full, she liked to climb out and sit on the roof, imagining how much fun it would be if she could launch herself off on a broomstick. This always made Marie Claire nervous, but she didn't need to know. All Cat wanted to do was sit and eat her lemon bars and get the cake smell out of her hair.

The air felt cold as dry ice, thick and still, as if it were holding its breath, waiting for something to happen. Cat picked her way slowly around to the chimney pot. She sat down and leaned up against it. Taking the lemon bars out of their paper bag, Cat laid one on top of the bag and took a bite out of the other. Usually these were her favorites, but today they tasted too sweet and cloying. Her mother hadn't put enough lemon juice in, which was most unlike her, and Cat pushed the bag away with a sigh. Even being up here wasn't calming Cat down the way it always did. Her skin prickled and she wished the wind would blow. The heavy stillness felt ominous, and after a few moments, Cat realized why. There were no squirrels skittering up and down trees, gathering the last of the autumn nuts, no birds outside the bakery, pecking at the cake crumbs Marie Claire always scattered for them. Even the canal was silent, without the gentle splash of fish breaking the surface to feed. It was as if they had all gone into hiding. A gray wash covered the landscape, growing darker and grayer by the minute. And suddenly it didn't feel safe to be sitting out here.

Cat sensed something was about to happen right before the air started to crackle and fizz and a swarm of birds flew out of the trees on the opposite side of the canal. They lifted into the air like a black cloud, dropping feathers and cawing loudly before swarming out of sight.

Quickly Cat scrambled to her feet, her heart pounding fast. Something was out there in the woods. Something had scared all those birds.

A jagged bolt of lightning lit up the sky. There was no thunder to accompany it, and the lightning wasn't like any lightning Cat had ever seen before. Little green sparks flew off it, zooming across the sky and exploding into puffs of green smoke.

She had to get back inside, but just then the wind started to blow, howling over the rooftop with such force Cat worried she'd be swept over the edge. This was no normal wind, and she clung on to the chimney pot as mini tornados swirled out of the woods, tearing off down the canal and sending water splashing over the sides.

A thick black cloud appeared through the trees, and from the center of it flapped a giant bird. At least that's what it looked like. At first Cat thought it was an eagle, an enormous bald-headed eagle, hunched over with jutting wings.

But as the thing rose higher, Cat realized that it wasn't a bird at all. The dark, shadowy creature flying over the canal was a person clinging on to a broom, an outdoor work broom with a wide head of bristles. It was difficult to see what the person looked like from this distance, but Cat knew, without a doubt, that it was Madeline Reynolds.

Still clutching the chimney pot, Cat struggled to crouch down behind it, battling against the wind. The broomstick started to hover, and then, without any warning it swooped sharply toward her. Cat bit back a cry and held her breath, as if this might make her invisible. She felt a rush of frigid air as the broomstick flew nearer, and a dark shadow passed over Cat's head.

The wind dropped as suddenly as it had blown up. There was a flapping sound, and the atmosphere crackled with electricity as the witch landed a few feet away. A wild, ragged howl cut through the air, and Cat's stomach clenched in fear. She didn't move a muscle, not wanting to draw attention to herself. She could hear a rustling noise and then the sound of someone chewing.

Daring to look, Cat peeked around the chimney pot, and there, squatting on the roof, gobbling down Cat's abandoned lemon bars, was an ancient bald-headed woman with a face like a shriveled walnut. It was the same face Cat had seen in the newspaper, the face of Madeline Reynolds. She chewed with her mouth open, shoving down the two lemon bars as if she hadn't eaten in a while. A large number ten was printed on the front of her boilersuit.

Cat shoved her fist in her mouth, biting down on a finger. She mustn't scream. She had to stay calm. This was an old woman called Maddie, that was all. If only Cat had her wand with her though. Right now would be the perfect moment to jump out and zap the runaway witch. But the wand was tucked away at the back of Cat's sock drawer.

There was a slurping sound as Madeline Reynolds licked her fingers clean. Cat was just contemplating throwing a roof slate at her when the old woman tipped back her head and howled, another raw, terrifying howl that made Cat think of wolves. Giving one more long howl, Madeline Reynolds sent a bolt of lightning ripping across the sky.

Then, without even glancing in Cat's direction,

she got back on her broom and took right off again, flying toward Potts Bottom. *Of course Peter had been right*, Cat thought. Madeline Reynolds was going back to Ruthersfield Academy. Maybe she planned to blow up the school? Cat didn't know. But she couldn't let her fear stand in her way. This was her chance to show Ms. Roach what she was capable of.

Not bothering to go carefully, Cat sped around the roof and slid in through her bedroom window. Even if Peter was still mad at her, she had to tell him what she'd just seen. As Cat picked up the walkie-talkie, it crackled to life.

"Cat, are you there?" Peter said, his voice so full of static it was difficult to hear. "My homemade barometer just burst. The can exploded. It expands when the pressure is low, but this is crazy." He sounded breathless. "Something's going on, Cat. I can sense it in the air."

Cat pressed the speak button. Her heart was beating so hard, she could feel it pounding against her rib cage. "You're right, Peter. I've just seen Madeline Reynolds. It looks like she's heading for Ruthersfield." There was a huge amount of static, and then Peter said something jumbled that Cat couldn't hear, followed by more static.

"What?" Cat dug the magic wand out of her sock drawer and tucked it into her pocket. She pulled her sweater down over it. "Peter, are you there?"

The receiver crackled back to life. "You're not still planning to try to catch her, are you?"

"I am," Cat replied. "Over and out." She threw the handset onto her bed and hurried downstairs. Cat slipped on her jacket and poked her head around the kitchen door. "I'm going up to Peter's if that's all right," she announced.

Her mother was sitting at the table listening to the radio. "That's fine," Poppy said, sounding distracted.

Marie Claire looked up from her book. "Did you hear the screech owl? It sounded like it was on the roof of the bakery."

"I did." Cat nodded.

"Well, be careful. There's quite a storm blowing out there," Marie Claire said.

"There's a storm brewing off the coast of Italy, too," Poppy added. "They think Madeline Reynolds is about to strike."

"I have a strong feeling she is," Cat agreed, noticing that her mother had stuck the postcard her dad had sent her to the fridge. Taking it down, Cat slipped the card into her pocket with the wand. She needed all the good omens she could get.

The streets of Potts Bottom were empty. Everyone was inside, Cat guessed, glued to their televisions and radios. As she ran toward Ruthersfield, the wind picked up again, swirling and gusting around her. Cat kept her head down as a buffer. She shivered inside her coat, fear and adrenaline coursing through her. To keep herself focused, she practiced saying "Intratangledcacoono" over and over again. Cat was so involved in her spell chanting that she didn't see the figure lurking by the academy gates until it stepped out of the gloom in front of her. With a soft cry of terror, Cat reached for her wand, realizing as she did so that the hunched over person in the long green raincoat was Peter. "I could have tied you up," Cat gasped, lowering her wand. "What are you doing here, Peter?"

"I thought you might need a little help." Peter said, holding up a coil of rope. "You can't face Madeline Reynolds without a backup plan, can you? Remember the summer your dad taught us lassoing? Well, I'm quite a good aim, if you recall."

Cat smiled so hard her cheeks ached. "I can't believe you came!"

"Well, your mum and my mum would kill me if anything happened to you, Cat. I mean, I couldn't sit at home and let you face Madeline Reynolds by yourself."

"Maddie," Cat reminded him. "Think of her as Maddie, Peter. And I'm so pleased you're here. I really am."

Peter shrugged. "You can be extremely annoying, Cat, but I'd hate to see you get hurt."

Cat gave him a slippery hug through his raincoat. "I'll take that as a compliment. You didn't tell your dad though, did you? We can go right to Uncle Tom's after we catch her. I just don't want the police charging in and wrecking everything."

"I thought about it," Peter confessed. "I almost did tell him, but he was staring at the television and, well . . ." He smiled at Cat. "I've no idea why I think this, because it makes absolutely no sense, but I sort of believe you can do it."

"Thanks, Peter." Cat's face grew warm, and she suddenly felt shy. To hide her emotions, her voice became extra efficient. "This is locked," Cat said, trying to push open the gate. "We're going to have to climb over the wall."

"Are you sure she's in there?" Peter asked, joining his hands together and holding them out so Cat could use them as a step to hoist herself up with.

"I'm certain of it," Cat panted. She sat on top of the wall, steadying herself with one hand and putting the other down to help pull Peter up. Then, scooting around to face the academy, they both dropped carefully to the playground, remembering to land with bent knees.

"Look." Cat nudged Peter. Hovering above Ruthersfield was the biggest storm cloud Cat had ever seen. It was black as thunder and swollen with rage, hanging inches above the roof.

"She's definitely in there," Cat said.

Chapter Twenty

··

Dark Magic

IT WASN'T AS DIFFICULT GETTING INSIDE THE ACADEMY as Cat had imagined. The front door was locked, of course, but around the back of the building they found a wide-open window, thin streams of black smoke leaking out of it. Not hot fire smoke. This smoke brushed against Cat like a cold caress, chilling her right down to her toes.

"Well, we know how she got in, don't we?" Peter whispered, looking about as frightened as Cat felt. She wondered if she should tell him to go home. After all, this had been her idea. But the truth was she wanted Peter here with her. She needed him beside her, making her be the brave one. Without him she might not have the courage to face Madeline Reynolds.

"Don't worry," Cat said in her most reassuring voice. "She really didn't look that dangerous, Peter. Just an old hunched woman with no hair."

They climbed through the window into what was clearly a classroom, shivering from the icy, smoking cold. Cat held out her hand and Peter took it, both of them giving the other strength. "Try to walk as quietly as you can," Cat whispered. "We want to be the ones to surprise her."

"Well, it's two against one, so the odds are in our favor," Peter said, which made Cat feel quite hopeful— until she looked at Peter's face and realized he was trying to make a joke.

"Come on." Cat squeezed Peter's hand, more for her benefit than his. "Follow me." They wove their way around rows of desks. A large crystal ball sat on the teacher's table, and a cabinet full of miniature crystal balls stood behind it. There was a poster of a hand on one wall, with dotted lines marked across the palm. *This must be the fortune-telling class,* Cat thought, and for a brief moment she imagined herself sitting at one of those desks, learning how to divine the future.

"Cat, are you all right?" Peter whispered, and Cat realized she had come to a stop.

"Yes, I'm fine." Cat shook her head. This was not the time to get all wistful and daydreamy. She couldn't afford to lose her focus.

Cat crept over to the door and opened it slowly, trying to stop any creaking. She peered out into the corridor, but it was dark and quiet, although plumes of smoke were drifting down the hallway to the left. "This way," Cat mouthed, motioning with her head. They tiptoed along following the curls of smoke. Cat stopped midstep as a tremendous crash exploded up ahead, followed by another colossal bang. Something buzzed from inside Peter's pocket, and he pulled out a small metal box with a red light flashing on the top.

"My earthquake detector," he whispered. "It works!"

"That is not an earthquake, Peter." Cat's eyes were huge, and she gripped Peter's fingers hard.

"But it picked up the vibrations, which is great." The sound of glass breaking shattered the air, and Peter's alarm started to buzz again.

"Will you turn that off?" Cat hissed, pulling him to a halt. "Right now!" Her whole body shook and it took all her willpower not to turn and run the other way. Suddenly, a whirlwind of black smoke swirled out of a classroom to their right. Cat glimpsed the bald head of Madeline Reynolds at the center of the tornado, and she watched in horror as the witch swept off down the corridor, not even glancing in their direction. What frightened Cat the most was that she had been clasping a wand. Not a difficult thing to find in a school for witchcraft, especially when you had been a student here for seven years and knew where the wands were kept.

Still holding hands, Cat and Peter walked up to the classroom leaking black smoke. They stood in the doorway staring at the destruction in front of them. "I think this was a spell room," Cat said, taking in the devastation. Tables and chairs had been upturned, cauldrons knocked over, and broken glass scattered everywhere. A pungent smell hung in the air, herbal and sweet, as spell ingredients pooled on the floor, their bottles smashed to smithereens.

"I don't think she has very good memories of this place," Peter murmured. "Your mum was right about that."

Until this moment, it hadn't occurred to Cat that maybe this was what her mother had been like, sweeping about in clouds of black smoke, causing destruction wherever she went. It was not a pleasant image, and for the first time Cat realized how sad her mother must have been. How hopeless she must have felt to behave in such a manner.

"Cat, are you all right?" Peter whispered again. "Because I'm fine to leave any time you want."

Cat shook her head. She turned and started walking down the corridor. If they didn't get this over with soon, she wasn't going to have the courage to go through with it. "Let's tie her up right now," Cat said, "before she does any more damage."

"Cat, what if your magic goes wrong?" Peter said. "I hate to bring this up, but I'm not sure I'm going to be able to lasso her. And could you please stop squeezing my hand quite so tightly?"

"You can't be a doubter," Cat whispered, trying to loosen her grip. "Clara Bell believes in me. I believe in me, and I need you to as well, Peter."

The trail of smoke led them down the hallway and up a flight of stairs. As they climbed, another huge crash sounded and Cat dropped Peter's hand, grabbing him by the arm. Being this brave was exhausting. The stairway lit up for a second as lightning streaked across the sky, and then a torrential downpouring of rain could be heard, pattering against the windows.

"It's just thunder," Cat said shakily. "From that cloud above the building."

"She's brewing a storm," Peter wailed softly. "She's going to wash Ruthersfield away, isn't she? She'll probably wash the whole of Potts Bottom away."

Cat could hear his teeth chattering. She forced herself

to remain calm. "I doubt our Maddie has that kind of power anymore," she said. She didn't really believe this at all, but she knew it was what Peter needed to hear. It was what she needed to hear too. "Come on, let's keep going," Cat said, giving him her best attempt at a smile.

They followed the smoke up to the third floor and along another hallway, passing two more classrooms, another laboratory, and a narrow purple door with BROOM SUPPLY CLOSET on it. At the end of the corridor the smoke turned into a small classroom; beautiful scrollwork letters on a plaque above the door read HONORS STUDENTS. Cat wondered if this was Madeline Reynolds's old class. She and Peter hovered in the hallway keeping to one side, so Madeline Reynolds wouldn't see them. As Cat peeked through the opening, she didn't know what she expected to find, but it certainly wasn't the world's most evil witch sitting at a desk in the third row, staring straight ahead as if she were waiting for class to begin. She looked so small and frail and wrinkled. It was hard to believe that she was dangerous. They watched her open the desk and peer inside. Madeline Reynolds looked at whatever was in it for a long moment before closing the lid.

Then, with a howl of anger, she zapped her wand furiously around the room. Desks exploded, spilling out pens and papers in a haze of purple smoke. There was a cracking sound and the blackboard shattered into pieces, crumbling to the floor as if it were a broken jigsaw puzzle. Posters melted off the walls, and a shelf of books flew into the air, the pages ripping loose, fluttering down like confetti.

Surveying her destruction, Madeline Reynolds seemed to slump, as if she had run out of energy. With a raspy sigh, she rested her bald head on top of the desk. Hunched over in her boilersuit, she looked like a bag of bones.

"I think she's taking a nap," Peter mouthed after four or five minutes had gone by. A soft, snoring noise could be heard, and Cat nodded in agreement. This was the time to catch her.

"Right, I'm going in," Cat whispered, stepping bravely through the door. She walked up to the teacher's desk with Peter right behind her. Madeline Reynolds lifted her head off the desk, staring straight at Cat. Her eyes were rheumy and unfocused, and she seemed a little disoriented.

"Do it," Peter whispered. "Now!"

But Cat completely froze. This was Madeline Reynolds in front of her. Madeline Reynolds who had given her nightmares for years. Cat felt her courage slip away like quicksand. She held the wand in her hand, but her arm wouldn't move and she couldn't remember the spell. Panic buzzed in Cat's ears, and she stared at the witch, paralyzed with fear. For a brief moment Madeline Reynolds looked startled at seeing anyone else in the room. She abruptly pushed her chair back, and something vulnerable passed through the old witch's eyes. Then they grew hard and angry, fixed on Cat with such hatred that Cat gave a silent plea, her legs turning soft as molasses.

"Cat, the spell," Peter cried, but although Cat heard him, her brain wasn't responding. She watched in a trance as Madeline Reynolds flung the desk aside, looking like a wild animal as she overturned it. "Maddie," Peter croaked in a hoarse voice, "can we talk about this?"

The old witch pointed her wand at them, sending out a jagged bolt of lightning. And that's when Cat screamed.

Peter pushed her to the floor as the lightning whizzed over their heads, singeing his frizzy hair. "Get under the desk, Cat," he said, fumbling for the rope. "I should have stayed home and watched television. That would have been so much smarter."

He scrambled back up and waved the lasso once around his head, then let it fly toward Madeline Reynolds. It was a good aim. A really fantastic aim. And for a second Cat thought it was going to reach its target. But the old witch sent out another lightning bolt, which met the rope in midair.

"Awwwh!" Peter screamed, as a zigzag current of electricity traveled up the rope, sending him stumbling backward. His hair stood on end and his body glowed green for a second. He was unable to hold on to the lasso, and it jerked out of his hands, flew across the room, and deftly tied itself into a knot. Baring her teeth, Madeline Reynolds hissed with loathing.

"Get over here," Cat sobbed, waving Peter back under the desk. "This was such a bad idea." Her mind had gone completely blank and she couldn't think what to do. But she had to get to Peter, who appeared to be suffering from shock, slumped on the floor and still glowing faintly green. Crawling toward him, Cat saw Madeline Reynolds raise her wand in the air again. "Hurry, Peter, grab my hand," Cat screamed, as the witch let fly a jumble of words.

But it was too late. Jagged lightning bolts shot toward them, and Cat dived back under the table. There was a burst of orange smoke where Peter had been sitting, followed by a powerful smell of wet fur. As the smoke cleared Cat saw a ginger-and-white guinea pig cowering behind a pair of wire-rimmed glasses. The glasses belonged to Peter. . . .

But Peter was nowhere in sight.

It took Cat a moment to understand what had happened, and as the truth slowly sank in, she covered her mouth in shock. Peter had been turned into a guinea pig. Cat watched him scuttle under the supply cupboard. A sick, dizzy feeling swept over her, followed by a powerful wave of fury. It was like watching your friend disappear down a drain, or vanish into a black hole. You couldn't quite believe he was gone.

"How dare you," Cat screamed, leaping to her feet and staring right at Madeline Reynolds. She had never felt this sort of rage before, flooding through her in a red-hot torrent, like a volcano about to explode. Cat wasn't scared anymore. Not one tiny bit. She was furious, and waving her wand in a fast spiral motion, she yelled, "Intratangledcacoono" at the top of her lungs.

At the same moment Madeline Reynolds pointed her wand at Cat, but Cat was too fast for her. She jumped out of the way as the lightning bolt zipped by, hitting a terrarium of frogs on a table behind her. Cat heard glass shattering, but she didn't look round because she was watching streams of white thread shoot out of her wand and spin toward Madeline Reynolds. The old witch couldn't move quickly enough, and in a matter of seconds, the threads wound around her from the shoulders down, tying her up in a sticky white cocoon. Her arms were bound to her sides and her legs pressed together. The only visible part of Madeline Reynolds was her head, which looked as small and withered as an old apple. She gave Cat a long, cold stare before closing her eyes. There was no fear in the old witch's face. Just a deep, fierce hatred, although for a moment before her lids drooped, Cat was sure she glimpsed sadness as well.

"Serves you right!" Cat said shakily, sinking down on the teacher's chair. She felt so light-headed she thought she might faint. Frogs were hopping everywhere, but Cat ignored them. She gave a soft sob, taking no pride in the fact that her spell had worked brilliantly. What did it matter? She had risked Peter's life and now he was a guinea pig. Who knew if she'd even be able to find him again? Peter had believed in her, and she had let him down. She had failed her friend in the worst way.

Cat gave her nose a hard blow. Sitting and crying wasn't going to help matters when she should be looking for Peter. His glasses were still on the floor, and Cat picked them up as she walked over to the supply cupboard, slipping them into her pocket for safekeeping. She bent down and peered underneath the cabinet. "Peter, are you there?" Cat called out. There was no answer, which was not surprising considering Peter was now a guinea pig.

It was also difficult to see much. The only light in

the room came from outside, and Cat looked around for a light switch. She couldn't see one, but there was a lamp on the teacher's desk. Trying not to step on frogs, Cat hurried over and unplugged it, carrying it back to the supply cupboard. She plugged it in again and shone the lamp under the cabinet, and there, cowering against the back wall, was Peter.

"It's all right," Cat said, using her gentlest voice. "Don't be scared. I've tied her up so she can't escape." Peter didn't move from his spot, but Cat was sure he shook his furry little head. "Honestly, Peter. It's quite safe. Please come out." Cat was just thinking about using a long pole or something to prod him out with, when two of the escaped frogs hopped underneath the cabinet. They were about the same size as Peter. As soon as he saw them, he gave a series of little squeaks and charged toward Cat, his ginger bottom swaying as he ran.

Cat scooped him up and gave his whiskery little face a kiss. She stared into the guinea pig's shiny currant eyes. "I will figure this out, Peter. I promise." She kissed his nose again. How Cat was going to figure this out she had no idea. But one thing was clear. She couldn't take Madeline Reynolds directly to Uncle Tom's, not with Peter being a guinea pig. Auntie Charlie and Uncle Tom would be devastated. Peter was their only child, and even though they were very fond of guinea pigs, they would not appreciate having Peter as one.

"I'm going to take you both with me to the bakery," Cat whispered. "Then I'll find my spell book and work out how to change you back." Peter gave a series of high-pitched little squeaks that sounded a lot like panic to Cat. "Don't be scared, Peter. You have to trust me," Cat whispered, slipping the guinea pig into her pocket.

He gave her finger a little nip and it wasn't entirely friendly. But Cat couldn't blame him for being upset. He probably knew that the odds of Cat Campbell changing him back into a boy again were not good. Not good at all.

Chapter Twenty-One

....

An Unusual Journey

THE NEXT BIG PROBLEM CAT FACED WAS HOW TO GET Madeline Reynolds and a guinea pig back to the bakery by herself. The storm was still blowing outside the windows but not as hard as before. There were long pauses between the rumbles of thunder, and the rain seemed to be letting up.

Cat walked over to Madeline Reynolds, who appeared to have drifted off to sleep again. She wondered how heavy the witch was. Cat hated touching her, but there was no other choice. Just in case Madeline Reynolds started screaming, or tried to bite her, Cat took a roll of sparkly purple duct tape out of the supply cupboard and, grimacing in disgust, she taped the witch's mouth shut. Madeline Reynolds's skin was as soft and wrinkled as moldy citrus peel, and she stank of rotten grapefruit and old porridge. Turning her head to one side so as not to breathe in the stench, Cat wrapped her arms around Madeline Reynolds and tried to lift her up. It was impossible. She might be a bag of bones, but she was still too heavy for Cat to carry.

Walking around the witch, Cat studied her from all angles. There was a nice loop of white thread for grabbing on to in the middle of Madeline Reynolds's back, and for a brief moment Cat felt a glimmer of satisfaction at how perfectly the spell had worked. If this had been performed on a screaming toddler lying in the street, you could simply pick the toddler up by the loop and cart him back home for a bath. Cat tried picking Madeline Reynolds up this way, but she still couldn't get her off the ground.

"There has to be a solution," Cat said, speaking to Peter as if he was right beside her. Just because he happened to be a guinea pig didn't mean she intended to ignore him. Cat paced around the room, stepping over bits of broken desk. A large glossy poster lay crumpled on the floor, and she stopped in front of it. The poster showed a sketch of a young girl riding on a broomstick, her back straight, and her legs tucked underneath her. At the top in bold letters, it read, "Correct Posture for Broomstick Riding."

"Hey, I have an idea, Peter," Cat said, her enthusiasm starting to return. She ran out into the hallway and found the door with BROOM SUPPLY CLOSET on the front. Flinging it open, Cat switched on the light. She stepped inside, staring at the neat rows of broomsticks hanging from the wall. There were Beginner Brooms, Easy Flyers, and High Strung Stallions. Then a whole row devoted to Stunt Brooms, Sport Brooms, and Work Brooms. Cat reached for a Stunt Broom but changed her mind with a sigh. This was not the time for stunts. She hung it back up and took down a Beginner Broom, but as she did so, Cat noticed a bin in the corner of the closet full of chunky-looking broomsticks. The notice on the wall said "Training Brooms," and Cat tugged one out of the barrel. It didn't look fast or sleek like the High Strung Stallion, or up for much in the way of tricks like the Stunt Broom, but Cat guessed this was her best chance of getting them all home safely. The broom had an on-off switch, and Cat realized it was motorized, which accounted for its thick, chunky shape. *This must be the equivalent of riding a bike with training wheels,* she guessed. Anyone could do it, or that's what she hoped.

Cat dragged the broom back into the classroom, trying not to think about how many rules she must be breaking. Uncle Tom would probably lock her up for trespassing on school property, using magic without permission, stealing a broomstick—not to mention the fact that she was completely responsible for his son being turned into a guinea pig. Cat might not have cast the spell on Peter, but he would never have been here in the first place if it weren't for her.

Madeline Reynolds was still snoring away. Her head had nodded forward and she looked like a giant white slug. Cat walked around behind her and poked the end of the broomstick through the loop of string. Then she put one leg over and flicked the switch to on, grasping the handle in both hands.

Peter started to squeak, poking his nose out of her pocket and looking up at Cat with terrified eyes. She knew exactly what he was thinking, and she felt terrible. "I'm sorry, Peter. I know this isn't going to be fun, but there's no other way." Peter did some more high-pitched shrieking. "Just close your eyes," Cat suggested. "Don't look down."

The broomstick started to vibrate, and Cat pointed the nose upward. She could feel Peter trembling in her pocket. With a sudden jerky motion, they rose into the air, Madeline Reynolds dangling underneath. Cat flew bumpily around the room, gasping and laughing at the same time. She realized she hadn't opened a window, and not wanting to get off now that they were airborne, Cat directed the broomstick toward the door, flying through it into the hallway. They would just have to go back the way they had come.

There was a button for speed, and Cat turned it to the lowest setting as they flew down the stairs. Going down was much more difficult to control than going up, Cat realized, and she almost fell off, bumping into the wall and steadying herself against the banister with her foot. Peter was rustling around and nipping at her thigh, which made it difficult for Cat to concentrate. Plus, she worried he might try to jump out. The extra weight beneath the broomstick didn't help matters either, but Cat navigated her way along the ground-floor corridor and into the fortune-telling classroom. She wobbled above the rows of desks and out the open window.

It was still raining, and the wind buffeted Cat about. Flying at night was hard enough without having to battle bad weather. As she gained height, the broom's automatic headlamps switched on, so at least Cat could see where she was going. She rose steadily into the sky, leveling out at about twenty feet above the rooftops. Cat wasn't too worried about being seen. None of the villagers would be out in this weather, and she was quite certain they were all glued to their television sets. She gripped the handle tight, trying her best to fly smoothly. It was not all that easy because they kept hitting wind pockets and getting tossed about. Every time this happened Madeline Reynolds slid along the handle, and Cat struggled to keep the broomstick as horizontal as she could manage to stop the witch from sliding off.

Cat focused on the landscape beneath her. She couldn't afford to overshoot the bakery and get lost. Luckily the broomstick headlamps reflected off the canal, and Cat flew along beside it until she saw the glow of lights coming from Poppy's. As she got closer, Cat could see that she had left her bedroom window open, but swooping through it would not be as easy as she'd anticipated. She had to circle the bakery twice before she got the broomstick lined up properly, and, gritting her teeth in concentration, Cat finally flew through. Having no idea how to land, she nosedived onto the bed, where she bounced once and rolled right off onto the floor.

Cat lay still for a moment, waiting for the room to stop spinning. She had bumped her head, and touching a hand gingerly to the spot, Cat could already feel a lump forming.

"Cat, is that you?" Poppy called up the stairs. "I thought you were at Peter's. What on earth are you doing, banging around up there?"

"I dropped something," Cat shouted, getting slowly to her feet. She was relieved to see that Madeline Reynolds had arrived in one piece. The witch had slipped off the broomstick and was lying on Cat's bed with her eyes closed—though Cat sensed she wasn't asleep. Staggering over to the door, her legs all stiff and shaky, Cat called out, "I just got in. I came right up."

"You weren't going to say hello first?" Cat could hear the hurt in her mother's voice.

"I'm tired, Mamma."

"It sounds like they're getting close to catching Madeline Reynolds," Poppy said. "No sightings yet, but the storm looks as if it's going to be a big one, and she's bound to be somewhere behind it. They've got fifty thousand different units lined up and waiting."

"Really," Cat called down, thinking that grown-ups could be just the tiniest bit thick sometimes. She knew Peter would be laughing his head off if he weren't a guinea pig, and Cat patted her pocket to see how he was doing. She patted it again, more wildly this time, and then shoved her hand inside, feeling frantically about. "Oh no!" Cat groaned, stuffing both hands in both pockets and turning them inside out. Peter's glasses were there but not Peter. Somewhere between here and Ruthersfield her friend must have fallen out.

Cat had been holding herself together for so long, but she couldn't do it anymore. Walking numbly back into her room, she sank down on the floor and started to cry. Soft, quiet tears that dripped onto the rug. She was so involved in her crying that she didn't hear the little chomping sound right away. It took Cat a few minutes to notice that a ginger-and-white guinea pig was chewing the frayed edges of her jeans.

Chapter Twenty-Two

························

Cold and Gloomy

TO KEEP PETER SAFE, CAT PUT HIM IN HER SOCK DRAWER.
She left the drawer open so he could have some air,
and right away he made himself a nest in the corner,
snuggling down on her green woolly tights. "That was
really scary," Cat said, stroking his furry back. He made
a happy little chattering sound. "I thought I'd lost you
for good." Cat realized that Peter must have crawled
out of her pocket after landing, when she was lying on
the floor, and she couldn't risk anything else happening
to him until she had turned him back into a boy.

"I'm going to go and find the spell books my mum
hid," Cat whispered, feeling bad about leaving him

alone in the same room with Madeline Reynolds. The witch had opened her eyes, and every time Cat glanced in her direction, she was shocked by the emptiness she saw. It was as if Madeline Reynolds had lost her soul. Even the hatred and fury from earlier had leaked away. Cat felt like she was looking at a shell, a shell with nothing inside.

"I won't be long," Cat whispered, breaking bits of a Twirlie bar and scattering them in front of Peter. "This is much more tasty than my tights."

Cat crept into her parents' bedroom, trying not to make a noise. It had occurred to her that Auntie Charlie and Uncle Tom might be wondering where Peter was, and picking up the extension by her parents' bed, Cat quickly dialed their number. She was relieved when Auntie Charlie answered. Uncle Tom, being a policeman, might have been able to tell that Cat was hiding something.

"Auntie Charlie, it's Cat. Peter was wondering if he could sleep over," Cat said, trying to keep her voice down. "It's all right with my mum if it's all right with you."

"Oh, yes, that's fine," Auntie Charlie agreed. "Just don't stay up too late chattering!"

Well, at least she didn't have to worry about Peter's parents until morning now. Cat hung up the phone and peered under the bed, but there was nothing to see except dust balls. Then she searched in the closet, even standing on a chair so she could reach the top shelf. One by one she pulled open all the drawers in the carved rosewood bureau her father had brought back from Africa on one of his trips. She felt among the sweaters and T-shirts, but the books were not in there. They weren't in the linen cupboard either. Cat didn't think her mother would have put them in Marie Claire's room, so they had to be downstairs.

The fire had gone out, Cat noticed as she walked into the kitchen. Marie Claire was rocking in her chair beside it, while Cat's mother sat hunched over the table.

"Why are you sitting in the dark?" Cat said in surprise. Well, it wasn't quite the dark. One small lamp shone from the sideboard, but with no fire burning and nothing in the oven, the effect was cold and gloomy. Cat switched on all the overhead lights. "Do you want me to start the fire again, Marie Claire?"

"Don't bother, Cat. I'm going to go to bed."

"We should all go to bed," Poppy said with a yawn. "And when we wake up tomorrow, the worry will be over and Madeline Reynolds will have been caught."

"I should think that's very likely!" Cat couldn't help saying.

"There's soup on the stove if you want some." Poppy

sighed, rubbing her hands across her face. "Marie Claire and I had a bowl earlier."

Cat shook her head. "No, thank you." She walked around the room, opening cupboards and looking inside.

"Have you lost something, *chérie*?" Marie Claire asked, watching Cat study the shelf of cookbooks. It would be just like her mother to hide the magic books in with her cookbooks.

"Mmmm, a study guide I need for homework," Cat said. Not meeting Marie Claire's gaze, she turned and hurried out of the kitchen. Cat was not a good liar, and she could feel her face grow warm as she shut the door softly behind her. They had to be somewhere, Cat thought as she darted across the hall into the bakery. It was the only place besides Marie Claire's room she hadn't looked. But after poking around for a few minutes, checking in the drawers that held all the cake boxes and ribbon and pretty tissue paper, it was clear that the books weren't in there. Cat was about to go back upstairs and check on Peter when she realized she hadn't looked in the coat cupboard. Creeping out into the hall, Cat softly pulled open the closet door, and there, hidden at the back behind the winter coats and jackets, she found her cardboard box of books.

"Score," Cat whispered, tugging them out. She glanced at the kitchen door, but it was still closed.

Hugging the box of books against her chest, Cat tiptoed up to her room.

She averted her head as she walked in, not wanting to see Madeline Reynolds. The witch was still lying on Cat's bed, silent and motionless, but just being in the same room with her was awful. Cat could feel Madeline Reynolds's presence even when she wasn't looking at her, as if her very evilness was poisoning the air. It had to be at least ten degrees colder in the room than the rest of the cottage, and Cat put on an extra sweater. She propped a chair in front of her door since it didn't have a lock; she needed warning if her mother came up.

Then she knelt on the rug with *Practical Magic* open in front of her and leafed through it. There was nothing that seemed likely to change Peter back. Most of the spells were basic ones. Making an object move, making an object levitate, a simple color change spell, mixing a basic potion. Cat sighed and shut the book, guessing that what she needed was probably in *Advanced Magic*.

As she reached for the volume, Cat could sense Madeline Reynolds's eyes on her. It was so unnerving being this close to the witch, and unable to stop herself, Cat looked up. Madeline Reynolds was staring right at her. With a soft cry, Cat quickly turned away, remembering what had happened to the guard at Scrubs. What if Madeline Reynolds decided to hypnotize her?

Even though she wanted to run out of the room, Cat forced herself to stay put, thumbing through the pages of *Advanced Magic*. Sure enough, at the back of the book she found what she was looking for. Under the heading "Emergency Action," Cat discovered a list of reversal spells, including "How to reverse a shape shift spell."

"This sort of magic should not be attempted by the novice witch," Cat read. "In the unfortunate circumstances that a hex has been performed—*which is highly illegal and against the code of magic*—it is necessary to know how to undo it. Proceed with caution and only if no other option is available."

Well, no other option was available, so Cat would just have to give it a go.

"It's going to be fine, Peter," she reassured him, lifting the guinea pig out of her sock drawer. Her heart was racing at the thought of performing such a spell, especially since Cat knew she was most definitely still a novice. Even though she had managed to tie up Madeline Reynolds, this sort of magic was far more complex and, Cat strongly suspected, beyond her capabilities. But she had to try. Poor Peter couldn't stay a guinea pig forever. If she believed she could do this, then maybe the spell would work.

"Don't worry," Cat whispered. She stroked Peter's fur and put him gently on the floor. "You'll be back to normal in no time." Cat read the spell through carefully five times. She polished her wand, wriggled into a more comfortable position, and took some deep slow breaths, trying to calm herself down. Peter seemed to be getting impatient. He was nibbling at the rug and squeaking loudly. "Right, I'm ready," Cat finally said, hoping she wouldn't make the situation worse. She waved her wand from left to right, performing the little flick at the end as the picture in the book demonstrated. "Ficklebacklerumpusright," Cat sang out, chanting the spell with emphasis on the first and last syllables.

There was a cloud of pink smoke and a faint smell of hamburgers. At first Cat thought nothing had happened, because Peter ran around in circles, squeaking, and it took her a moment to realize that one of his little clawed feet was now human. A tiny human foot with perfectly shaped pink toes. "Oh, flipping fish cakes, I have made it worse," Cat gasped.

Peter scurried over and bit Cat on the foot, as if to say he did not approve of what she'd done at all. She yelped and pushed him gently away. "I don't blame you, Peter. I feel like biting me too."

"Cat?" Poppy knocked at the door. "Can I come in a moment?" she called softly.

"Uh, no! Not right now, Mamma. I'm talking to Peter. On our walkie-talkies," Cat added. "It's a private conversation."

"Well, I'm off to bed then," Poppy said, hesitating a few moments longer before calling out, "Good night."

"Night." Cat sighed, rubbing at her temples. She picked up the wand and put it down again, unsure what to do. She couldn't risk anything else going wrong. The last thing Cat wanted was to mess up Peter further. He already looked pretty odd with his little pink foot. This spell was way too advanced for her, and she knew in her heart she should not attempt it again. After dithering for another hour, Cat finally had to admit to herself that she wasn't going to be able to turn Peter back.

Chapter Twenty-Three

....

Kitchen Magic

FOR A LONG TIME, CAT SAT ON THE FLOOR WITH PETER curled up in her lap. "I'm so sorry," Cat whispered, stroking his furry back. "My magic just isn't good enough." She thought about asking Clara Bell for help, but Cat didn't want to get her into trouble. It wasn't fair to involve a Ruthersfield teacher in her mess. Besides, Cat had a strong suspicion that Clara Bell's magic would not be strong enough for this kind of spell either. There was only one person who might be able to help. But Cat didn't think she was brave enough to face her. "I have to though, don't I?" Cat whispered to the guinea pig. "For your sake, Peter."

She had always been there for Cat in the past, and if this problem wasn't connected with magic (which it most certainly was), there wouldn't be an issue. Not knowing whom else to turn to, Cat got up off the floor and put Peter back in her sock drawer, terrified of her mother's reaction.

"Mamma, are you awake?" Cat whispered, hovering over her mother's bed. She touched her lightly on the shoulder, and Poppy woke with a start.

"What is it? What's happening? Are you sick, Cat?"

"No," Cat whispered, feeling words stick in her throat.

Poppy leaned over and turned on her bedside light. She squinted at the clock. "It's the middle of the night."

"I know. Please come, Mamma," Cat said, and then in a quivery voice, she added, "I need you."

Without asking any more questions, Poppy got out of bed. While she slipped on her dressing gown and knotted the sash, Cat darted into her bedroom and scooped up Peter. They met in the hallway.

"This is the problem?" Poppy said, peering at the guinea pig in Cat's hands. "Isn't that one of Peter's?" She gave a sleepy yawn.

"No." Cat shook her head, holding him up so her mother could see the guinea pig's back foot. "It *is* Peter."

"Oh, my gracious!" Poppy gasped, staring at the foot. "What have you done?"

"I . . . Oh, Mamma," Cat whispered, unsure how to begin.

"Cat?"

"Madeline Reynolds turned him into a guinea pig, and I can't turn him back again," Cat blurted out. "I tried, but it didn't work very well." She gave her mother a pleading look. "That's why I need your help."

"Madeline Reynolds?" Poppy put a hand against the wall to steady herself. "Madeline Reynolds is near Italy, Cat. This is ridiculous," she said, starting to sound angry. "What are you playing at? What have you done to this poor creature? You found those books, and you've been mucking about with magic, haven't you?" Poppy's face had gone red, her neck mottled with splotchy color. "Does Peter know what you've done to his guinea pig?" she fumed. "Is he in here too?" Poppy stormed into Cat's bedroom and switched on the light. "Don't play me for stupid, Cat. I've had enough."

"Oh!" Poppy gasped, standing in the doorway. "Oh!" she said again, holding on to the doorknob. The silence was a long one as Poppy stared and stared at Madeline Reynolds, who appeared to have fallen asleep again. She put a hand to her mouth but still didn't speak.

"I caught her myself," Cat finally said. "With the Trapped like a Fly Spell."

"You did?" Poppy turned to her daughter. She shook her head in disbelief. "I cannot believe this. I thought you were terrified of Madeline Reynolds!"

"Well, I was, but in *The Late Bloomer's Guide to Magic* it says if I want to get my magic under control, I have to start by overcoming my fears. So I've been working on them," Cat said rather proudly. "Spiders, as well as Madeline Reynolds."

"I see," Poppy murmured faintly.

"And I couldn't have done it without Peter," Cat admitted. "At first I was terrified, but when Madeline Reynolds turned him into a guinea pig, I got so mad I wasn't scared at all anymore, and my spell worked beautifully."

"But I—I mean, where was she? How did you?"

"Ruthersfield," Cat explained. "It was you who helped Peter figure it out, Mamma. You said she probably hated school as much as you did, and he reckoned this is where she would come back to. The place her unhappiness began."

For the first time in a week, Poppy laughed. "Fifty thousand guards waiting to catch her, and

Cat Campbell does it alone. You are definitely your father's daughter." She paused a moment, her smile slipping away. "But why, Cat? Why would you do something so dangerous, so utterly stupid and dangerous?"

"Because I knew I'd never get my magic under control otherwise. This was the only way, if I wanted to get into Ruthersfield. I had to face my biggest fear. Plus," Cat said, smiling, "I figured it would impress Ms. Roach if I managed to catch Madeline Reynolds. She'd see how serious I am, and she'd have to offer me a place."

"You did this to get into Ruthersfield?"

"Are you mad at me?"

"I'm stunned," Poppy murmured, leaning against the wall. "And I need a serious cup of tea. Then we must call Uncle Tom."

"Mamma, no!" Cat looked horrified. "We can't call Uncle Tom yet. Not until you change Peter back."

"Wait just one second." Poppy held up her hands, her voice sober. "I can't do that, Cat. I've been banned from practicing magic ever again."

"But you have to," Cat insisted, blinking back her tears. "I found the books in the coat closet. The spell is in *Advanced Magic*, but it's too complicated. I tried once and look what happened." Cat nodded at Peter's foot. "I'm not good enough." She gave her mother a pleading look. "You have to try, Mamma. Auntie Charlie's your best friend. We can't let her see Peter like this." Cat held out her hands, and she and her mother both looked at Peter, who gave a little squeak, waving his foot in the air.

After a moment Poppy said, "No, you're right, we can't." Poppy gathered her hair over one shoulder and braided it quickly. "Get the spell book and bring him down to the kitchen." She glanced across at Madeline Reynolds. "Do you think she can escape?"

"No, definitely not," Cat said, unable to contain her grin. "The spell worked way better than I expected. She could never untie herself."

"So how did you get her home?" Poppy asked as they hurried down the stairs.

"I don't think you want to know, Mamma," Cat said. "Put it this way. Antonia Bigglesmith would be proud of me!"

Poppy made a space on the kitchen table, and Cat placed Peter next to a jar of walnuts. He ran right over to the electricity bill and started to nibble the envelope. "You'll need this, Mamma," Cat said, holding out Poppy's old novice wand.

"It's been so long since I did any magic," Poppy

said. She gave the wand a tentative wave. "Gosh, I hate these things. Even holding it makes me feel sick." Poppy shuddered. "All right, Cat, find me the page."

"It's a really difficult spell," Cat warned her, opening *Advanced Magic* to the back. "I mean, it looks easy, it sounds easy. But it's just so hard."

"Let me see." Poppy studied the page. She closed her eyes for a moment, took a deep breath and, waving her wand in the air, said, "Ficklebacklerumpusright." A burst of pink smoke covered the table, with showers of green sparkles shooting out like fireworks. And when the smoke cleared, there was Peter, looking rather dazed. He had knocked over the jar of walnuts, his legs sprawled across the kitchen table.

"Thanks, Auntie Poppy!" Peter said. "My mum was right. She always said you were great at magic."

"You are," Cat said rather wistfully. "You're fantastic, Mamma."

"But I have no passion for it." Poppy looked at her daughter. "And you do, Cat Campbell. I didn't realize until this moment just how much."

Peter nibbled on a walnut. His nose was still twitching. "Cat's bound to get in to Ruthersfield now, don't you think?"

"That's up to Ms. Roach," Poppy said. Her face

was guarded as she swept flakes of sparkly magic off the table, and Cat couldn't tell what her mother was thinking.

"But you'll let me reapply?" Cat asked. "Seriously, Mamma?"

"If it's really what you want, I'll support you." Cat squealed and turned a cartwheel. "But that doesn't mean what you did was okay," Poppy added. "It was dangerous and stupid and —"

"Pretty amazing," Peter said, slipping on his glasses. "Honestly, Cat, you were fantastic tonight."

"I was terrified to begin with, Peter. You were the really brave one."

"Well, it was totally worth getting turned into a guinea pig to watch you zap Madeline Reynolds. I had a great view from under the cupboard! Can't wait to see my dad's face when we tell him."

"Which will be in the morning," Poppy said firmly. "There's no need to disturb him now. Madeline Reynolds isn't going anywhere, and we all need to get some rest." Poppy glanced at the clock. "Not that there's much night left."

"Actually, I had quite a good nap in your sock drawer," Peter confessed. "Although I did nibble a hole in your green tights, Cat. I'm afraid I couldn't help myself."

"I'll put sleeping bags down in my room, and we can leave Madeline Reynolds where she is," Poppy said.

It was only as Cat drifted off to sleep on her mother's bedroom floor, that she wondered how smart a decision this was, leaving Madeline Reynolds alone next door.

Chapter Twenty-Four

Torrential Flood

C AT WOKE UP TO THE SOUND OF LOUD OPERA
music playing. She recognized the tune at once. It
was from *Carmen*, Marie Claire's favorite French opera, by
the composer Georges Bizet. Poppy and Peter were still
asleep, Poppy sprawled across her bed and Peter's frizzy
black hair poking out of his sleeping bag. Not wanting to
disturb them, Cat crept out into the hallway. She put her
ear to the door of her bedroom, but there was nothing to
hear, and so Cat hurried downstairs. Uncle Tom would
arrive soon. He could deal with Madeline Reynolds.

As Cat skipped into the kitchen, she could smell
crepes cooking.

"Good morning, *chérie*," Marie Claire sang. "It is a beautiful day, is it not? Finally the sun is shining." She gestured out the window, and Cat saw a family of winter swans floating down the canal. Little sparkles of light glittered on the water. The sky was wide and blue. "I wanted to wash all the sadness out of this bakery. Play my music. Loud!"

"It was wonderful to wake up to," Cat said, giving Marie Claire a hug. "I've missed hearing your music all week. And when Mamma comes down, we have a surprise for you!"

"Oh, I love surprises, especially nice ones!" Marie Claire said. "I couldn't listen anymore to that man on the radio. He is making us worry about things that might never happen, droning on and on in his miserable voice. I have had enough," Marie Claire declared, banging a wooden spoon down on the counter.

"That's just what the postman said," Cat told her.

"Well, Ted Roberts is a wise man." Marie Claire breathed deeply and poured batter into a pan. "Even my ankle feels better this morning."

"And you lit a fire," Cat said, warming her hands in front of the hearth.

"A fire is the heart of the home. So is the oven. When those stop going, then the home falls apart," Marie Claire said. "Yesterday was a bad day. But today we can start afresh." She picked up a spatula and flipped over the crepe. "I cannot bear to see you and your mother fighting, Cat. It breaks my old heart. You have to remember that I've known your mother since she was a little girl, and it wasn't easy for her. She struggled in a way you will never know. What Poppy went through is not anything I would ever wish on another person." Marie Claire flipped the crepe onto a plate and sprinkled it with lemon and sugar. She rolled it up and handed it to Cat. "Magic almost ruined her life, Cat. You need to remember that. It is why she's so against it."

"I know, Marie Claire." Cat nodded. "I think I'm beginning to understand."

"Well, that is excellent news!" Marie Claire said in satisfaction. "Now, sit down and eat your crepe. It is not good to eat wandering around like you do."

By the time Poppy and Peter came downstairs, Cat had devoured six crepes. They tasted much better than usual this morning, even better than her favorite toaster tarts, and Cat was just debating whether or not she should have a seventh when her mother walked over to the radio. "Do you mind if I turn this down, Marie Claire? Just a tiny bit," Poppy said. "It's lovely but so loud, and I need to hear the doorbell ring. I'm expecting Uncle Tom any second." She turned and smiled at Cat. "He couldn't believe it when I told him what you'd done, Cat. Does Marie Claire know yet?"

"No." Cat shook her head, feeling embarrassed. She didn't want a big fuss stirred up because of capturing Madeline Reynolds. That would make her so uncomfortable. She just wanted to get into Ruthersfield. "I was waiting for you and Peter."

It didn't matter anyway because Marie Claire wasn't paying the slightest attention to their conversation. She was standing by the oven, frowning up at the ceiling. "We have a leak, Poppy," she said, as a steady stream of water dripped down into her crepe pan.

"I think it's coming from Cat's room," Peter announced. "Maybe a pipe burst."

Water splashed onto the table. "It's dripping everywhere," Cat said, as a drop landed on her nose and dribbled into her mouth. "And it's salty," she added, with a growing sense of dread. "Like the ocean."

A steady stream of water was pouring onto the fridge, and Cat looked at her mother in horror. What on earth had they been thinking, leaving Madeline Reynolds alone all night long? Of course, something awful must have happened. Cat's magic probably hadn't been strong enough to keep her tied up, and she was, right at this very moment, brewing a huge sea storm in Cat's room. Without another word, Cat grabbed the magic wand off the table and dashed up the stairs after her mother.

"Shouldn't you wait for my dad?" Peter called after them. "You don't want to go in there without backup."

"Whatever's going on, I don't think the Potts Bottom police force could deal with it," Poppy said.

Cat raced past her mother. "Mamma, this is my mess," she panted. "Please let me go first."

"Honestly, Cat! Enough of the heroics." Poppy grabbed the wand out of Cat's hand. "Get behind me," she ordered. "I'm your mother, and you'll do as I say."

Cat had no idea what they were about to witness as her mother pushed opened her bedroom door. But nothing could have prepared her for the floods of water that gushed out, torrents and torrents of water, overflowing onto the bed and washing Madeline Reynolds straight toward them. She was still tied up tightly, but tears were coursing down her cheeks. The tape across her mouth had come loose, Cat saw, probably from all her crying. And Cat watched in amazement as Madeline Reynolds opened her mouth wide and started to sing, huskily at first, as if her throat needed oiling, but then with more and more strength. The sound grew richer and sweeter. Cat imagined melted honey being poured down her throat. An expression of stunned surprise shone from the old, wrinkled face. She looked as shocked as Cat and Poppy as she belted out the most beautiful song Cat had ever heard. It was the song still playing on the radio below, the sweet, soaring music of *Carmen*.

Sunlight poured in through the window, and rainbows danced on the walls as Madeline Reynolds swept past them, not on a wave of seawater, Cat realized, but riding her own salty tears. Tears spilled from the old witch's eyes, and music poured out of her mouth, as she floated down the cottage stairs. Splashing along behind, Cat and her mother followed Madeline Reynolds straight through to the bakery. Water filled the glass cases and pooled around Cat's legs. Years and years of locked away sadness finally let loose.

"*Mon Dieu*," Marie Claire murmured, coming to stand beside Cat. "Never have I heard such singing."

"It's Madeline Reynolds," Poppy whispered. "Cat caught her last night." She couldn't keep the pride from her voice, and Cat slipped her hand into her mother's.

"*Mon Dieu*," Marie Claire murmured again, leaning against Peter. "To think I should ever hear such a thing." She closed her eyes for a moment, and in the golden light of the bakery her face looked young again.

"This is how angels must sound," Cat said. She lost track of time as they stood and listened to Madeline Reynolds, singing the purest, sweetest music any of them had ever heard. It made Cat's insides ache with a longing for something that she couldn't identify.

When Uncle Tom arrived with five police cars full of officers, they splashed inside the bakery and immediately fell silent, their big boots shuffling to a stop. Mouths hung open and eyes glazed over as they listened to Madeline Reynolds, her voice filled with such heart and soul it brought joy to the toughest policeman. The problem was that as the old witch sang on, her tears kept falling and the water was now up to everyone's knees, not that they seemed to notice or care. When at last Madeline Reynolds fell silent, no one spoke for a while as the echo of her music lingered on.

"Well, I think I understand what has happened," Poppy said at last, wiping away her own tears. "Madeline Reynolds has found her passion again. *Carmen* has brought her back from the dark side."

"It was hearing such beautiful music," the old witch said, in a voice that hadn't been used for many years. "The singing was so exquisite." She sighed a deep, quivery sigh. "I felt like a dam inside me had burst, washing away my anger. All I ever wanted to do was sing."

Cat felt like she was looking at a different person. All the fury and hatred had gone from Madeline

Reynolds's face, and she stared around with big, fresh eyes as if seeing the world anew.

"Well, I'm afraid that's not going to be possible," Uncle Tom said. He cleared the surprise from his throat. "I've contacted Boris Regal, head officer at Scrubs, and you will be going back there today."

"Of course I will," Madeline Reynolds replied. She hung her head for a moment, her voice quavering. "I can never take back what I did to Italy. That is something I will have to live with always. And I am deeply ashamed of my actions. I shouldn't be let out of Scrubs Prison," she said sadly. "But I can sing every day for the rest of my life." And then with rather more force, Madeline added, "No one can take my music away from me ever again."

Uncle Tom flipped open a notebook and slid a pen out of his top pocket. "Ms. Reynolds," he said. "I'm going to need to ask you a few questions for my report. Is it true you broke into Ruthersfield Academy last night?"

"Yes, I did," Madeline answered with honesty. "I smashed up one of the spell labs."

"Was there a reason behind your behavior?"

Madeline nodded. "I've always hated the academy. My parents forced me to go there, but I couldn't stand magic. I wanted nothing to do with it."

"Just like me," Poppy whispered, and Cat squeezed her mother's hand.

"I loved to sing, but my parents wouldn't let me. They banned me from singing, if you can believe that."

"Oh, I can," Poppy said in agreement.

"So when I escaped, I wanted to go back to Ruthersfield and smash the place to pieces. Blow it right out to sea. I've been dreaming of doing that for years."

"And this young lady here tied you up?" Uncle Tom said, pointing at Cat with his pencil.

"She did indeed," Madeline said, and in a beautiful chanting voice, she sang, "That was a really brilliant spell you used!"

"Thanks." Cat blushed. "I can't take full credit for it, but thanks." She looked at Peter's dad. "Uncle Tom, can we untie her? I don't think Madeline Reynolds needs to be bound up like that anymore. Surely a pair of handcuffs would do."

"Oh, it's actually extremely comfortable," Madeline Reynolds said. "I feel like I'm being held in a big warm hug. This is the Trapped like a Fly Spell, if I'm correct."

"That's right," Cat said.

"Tantruming toddlers would just love this. It's like being wrapped up in your favorite blanket."

"You've got an excellent memory for spells," Cat said.

"Yes, I do." Madeline Reynolds gave a shaky sigh. "That's what made me so good. I never forgot a spell or mixed up my ingredients."

"One more question," Uncle Tom said, tapping his pencil against his pad. "What exactly did you have against Italy, Ms. Reynolds?"

A deep sadness brushed over the old witch's face. "I hate to remember that period," she whispered, her tears starting to flow again. "There was a music conservatory in Naples, run by Leonardo Di Messaverdi, the most wonderful singer of our time."

"Well, he was before he got washed away," one of the police officers muttered.

"You see, I'd been sent to study magic with the great Italian witch, Madame Russo. It was a huge honor to study with Madame Russo. My parents told me this over and over again. So did Ms. Norton, who was headmistress of Ruthersfield at the time." Madeline paused for a moment, looking straight at Cat's mother. "One day I was walking by the conservatory and I realized that I would never be able to follow my dream, and this sadness swept over me, so deep and profound, that before I knew what I was doing, I brewed an enormous storm and sent the bottom half of Italy out to sea."

"So you never planned to come back and do away with the top half then?" Uncle Tom asked.

"Good gracious me, no!" Madeline Reynolds sounded shocked. "Did anyone think I would?"

Peter started to laugh, and Uncle Tom clapped his hands. "Right, then, officers. Let's get this witch loaded up and sent back to Scrubs."

"Uncle Tom?" Cat beckoned to him, wading through Madeline's tears and leading Peter's dad upstairs. "Could you give this to Ms. Roach for me?" Cat handed him the training broom.

Uncle Tom frowned. "You flew on this?"

"I did, and I'm really sorry. I'm sure it breaks a gazillion laws, but I didn't know what else to do."

"You did good," Uncle Tom said gruffly. "I'm very impressed with you, Cat."

"If you could tell that to Ms. Roach, I'd love it. But I'd really like to keep what happened quiet with the press, if you don't mind. It would be awful if all these reporters and newscasters started showing up at the bakery. That's not what I want at all."

"You captured the most evil witch of the century," Uncle Tom said. "People are going to want to interview you, Cat."

"Yes, but wouldn't it be easier if the Potts Bottom Police Department handled it all? You can tell them whatever you like," Cat said. "I'm just a kid, Uncle Tom. I really don't want to be involved in all of this. So long as Ms. Roach knows what I did, I'm happy."

"Right, then." Uncle Tom pulled back his shoulders. "As chief of police I shall release a statement saying it was a top secret arrest, and any inquiries are being handled by me."

"You're the best, Uncle Tom," Cat said, grinning. "And try to convince Ms. Roach she shouldn't get too mad at me for taking a broomstick. I didn't know what else to do."

"How was it?" Uncle Tom asked as he splashed his way back downstairs. "Flying on this thing, I mean?" He waved the training broom in the air.

"It was fantastic." Cat sighed with real passion. "Best experience of my life."

Chapter Twenty-Five

·····································

If at First You Don't Succeed . . .

C AT'S GRANDPARENTS HAD INVITED THEMSELVES TO
tea that afternoon. The bakery was still a little
damp from all the water, but Uncle Tom had sent in the
fire department and they did an excellent job pumping
Madeline Reynolds's tears into the canal. There was
a faint salty tang in the air, which had inspired Poppy
to make a salted caramel cake, and she was busy melt-
ing butter and sugar together when Granny Edith and
Grandpa Roger came bustling into the kitchen.

"Where's our Cat?" Granny Edith said, holding her
arms out wide. Cat, who had been reading all about
magic in the Middle Ages, leapt up and gave her

grandmother a hug. "We are so proud of you, Catkins," Granny Edith said. "Not that it surprised either of us, did it, Roger?"

"No." Grandpa Roger laughed. "You're strong-headed, just like your mother." He walked over to the stove. "Whatever you're making, Poppy, it smells delicious."

"Wait, how did you know?" Cat said. "I asked Uncle Tom to keep it quiet."

"Oh, I won't say a word to anyone, don't worry." Edith lowered her voice. "Mrs. Plunket told me. Her son is on the force, so she heard all about it. And of course, being your grandparents, Cat, she thought we should know."

Cat could hear her mother chuckling at the stove. "You won't say anything will you?" Cat said. "I don't want a lot of fuss being made about it."

Granny Edith looked a touch guilty. "I did mention it to Maxine, I must admit. But she's my best friend, and she won't say a word."

"Oh, it will be all over the Ribbald Valley in no time!" Poppy said. "Telling Maxine is like telling the world!"

Granny Edith ignored this remark. "Anyway, Catkins, has Ms. Roach been in touch yet?"

"She called at lunchtime," Poppy said, "requesting

an interview with Cat on Wednesday. We're going up after school."

"Yes, and Mamma's coming with me," Cat said. "Ms. Roach told her she could!"

"Well, about time they changed those silly rules up there," Grandpa Roger said with a huff. "Our Poppy's been punished long enough."

Cat wore her mother's old Ruthersfield sweater for good luck. It still had a butter stain down the front that wouldn't wash out, but Cat didn't care. "You look lovely," Marie Claire told her, as Cat and her mother left the bakery.

"Yes, you do," Poppy said, taking her daughter's hand.

A flock of geese had landed by the canal, honking and pecking at the frozen ground. Cat stopped walking and stared down the path. Then she let go of her mother's hand and started to run, sending the geese scattering. "Daddy!" Cat screamed, flinging herself onto the man striding toward them. His hair was wild and curly, and he carried an enormous backpack. Swooping Cat up in his strong arms, he swung her around.

"You're just in time for my interview," Cat squealed.

"Tristram!" Poppy cried out, running over to her husband. Keeping a hold on Cat, Tristram swept

Poppy up in his arms as well. "My two favorite girls in the world!"

"I missed you so much," Cat said, and sighed, feeling his scratchy beard rub against her face. He smelled of high adventures, but neither Cat nor her mother minded. "Did you find the healing plant?" Cat asked.

"*Figius mantabelus*, but it took me a while," Tristram said. "I got lost in the mountains, stuck in a bog, and had to be rescued by one of the local tribes. They helped me locate the plant, which was situated in the northernmost tip of the country and took weeks to find." He shook his straggly hair. "Once you are out of the mountains, though, the mail service is rather good, and I sent clippings of it straight on to London for analysis, then headed home as fast as I could." Tristram added, "But the storms were terrible getting here! Unusual for this time of year."

"Yes, and I'll tell you why on the way, but we have to get to Ruthersfield," Cat said.

Leaving his backpack by the canal, Tristram grasped his wife by one hand and his daughter by the other, and they walked up to the academy together, Cat and Poppy filling him in on all the exciting things that had happened.

"You're going to be great," Poppy whispered, as they were shown into Ms. Roach's office. Cat could tell that her mother was nervous, because her hand was a little sweaty and she hadn't eaten anything for breakfast, which was most unlike her.

"Welcome," Ms. Roach said, glancing at Cat's dad in surprise. Her nostrils quivered, and she quickly opened the window. "Thank you all for coming."

Cat smiled eagerly and Poppy gave a small nod. Tristram Campbell pushed up his shirtsleeves and shook Ms. Roach heartily by the hand, showing off his hairy arms and compass tattoo.

"We have a lot to discuss," the headmistress went on, gesturing for the Campbells to sit down. She moved some papers around on her desk and clicked the end of her pen a few times. "What you did was extremely brave, Catherine. Because of you, Madeline Reynolds is now back behind bars. Not in the same high security cage, but safely out of harm's way."

"I don't think she's a threat anymore," Poppy said quietly.

Ms. Roach nodded in agreement. "They feel the same way at Scrubs. When I talked to Boris Regal, the head guard there, this morning, he told me they have moved Madeline into a comfy new wing. She's been singing nonstop since her return, much to the enjoyment of the other prisoners and the guards. In fact, they are setting up a recording studio for her in one of the huts," Ms. Roach said. "That way Madeline can share her music with the world."

"Oh, that's wonderful," Cat broke in. "She does have the most unbelievable voice."

"Yes, and all proceeds will go to rebuilding the bottom part of Italy," Ms. Roach said. She gave a small smile. "I'm told her first album will be released in time for Christmas."

"I'm so pleased," Poppy said. "She may still be in Scrubs, but at least she is doing what she loves."

"And isn't that what life's about?" Tristram added. "Doing what we love?"

Cat wiggled anxiously in her chair, wishing Ms. Roach would hurry up and say whether she was going to offer her a place.

"The authorities at Scrubs are examining how they house and treat their prisoners," Ms. Roach said. "Just as we are examining our entrance requirements here at Ruthersfield." The headmistress paused for a long moment, looking at Poppy, not Cat. "In the past it has been very difficult to determine what makes a witch go over to the dark side, simply because most witches do not return from there for us to ask them. Our approach has always been to scare the girls witless, make them understand what will happen if they do use black magic. But I'm not sure this is actually the best strategy," Ms.

Roach admitted. "I think we need to address the problem at the source, before it begins, to try to understand why a witch would abuse her powers. And with you and Madeline Reynolds, we now have a much better picture as to what went wrong."

"We both hated magic," Poppy said bluntly. "But nobody would listen to us." Tristram patted his wife's leg.

"Absolutely," Ms. Roach agreed. "Which is why we have decided to introduce a new exam for potential students. It will be called the Passion Quiz, and it will determine how much passion a girl has for her craft."

Poppy gave a short laugh. "Well, I would definitely fail that one!"

"Exactly, and so would Madeline Reynolds. Clearly this is an indicator that we can't ignore any longer." Ms. Roach gave a soft sigh. "I'm afraid Ruthersfield will lose a lot of very gifted students because they don't show the necessary passion needed to excel at witchcraft. But, and this is my hope," Ms. Roach said, "it should reduce the number of witches who turn evil."

"Well, I love that idea!" Cat said, clapping her hands.

Ms. Roach smiled. "In the passion department, Catherine, I have no worries about you, but"—her face grew serious—"there are other things that concern me."

"Like what?" Cat said, leaning forward. "I want this so much, Ms. Roach. You've no idea."

"Oh, I know how much this means to you, Catherine, believe me. But magic requires more than passion. It needs a cool head and an understanding of our rules." Ms. Roach leaned over her desk. "Capturing Madeline Reynolds was impressive, but it was also rash, impulsive, and quite honestly, very stupid. You put yourself in great danger, and I cannot have a student in this academy who acts with such hotheaded thoughtlessness."

"Sounds like Cat was extremely brave," Tristram said. "I'm proud of my daughter."

"It was certainly brave," Ms. Roach agreed, "but that is not the kind of courage we are looking for in our Ruthersfield girls."

Cat stared at Ms. Roach, feeling her dream finally start to slip away. She would never be a witch. That's what the headmistress was telling her.

"You cannot take the law into your own hands, Cat. Especially where witchcraft is concerned."

Cat tried to speak, but she knew if she opened her mouth, her voice would shake and she would cry. So she sat there, blinking and trying to swallow away the hard lump that had formed in her throat.

"Do you have any idea how hard Cat has worked

on controlling her magic?" Poppy said. "Please, Ms. Roach. You are never going to find a girl more passionate about magic than the one sitting in front of you. The reason she faced Madeline Reynolds is because this means so much to her." Poppy was trembling all over. "Please, give her a chance."

"She would make a fantastic witch," Tristram said, getting to his feet. "Thank you for your time, Ms. Roach, but I think you're making a big mistake."

"If you would let me finish," the headmistress said in her low, steady voice. She pressed a buzzer on her desk. "Could you send Ms. Bell in now, please?"

The door opened almost at once, and Clara Bell walked into the room, bringing with her the welcome scent of violets. "Clara Bell heads up the Late Bloomers program here at Ruthersfield," Ms. Roach said. "She's a big supporter of Catherine."

"Then it's a pleasure to meet you," Tristram said, giving Clara Bell his warmest smile.

"I have to be honest, Catherine," Ms. Roach continued, turning her attention back to Cat. "I was not going to give you another chance, but Ms. Bell here pleaded your case." The headmistress leaned back in her chair and folded her hands together. "She has convinced me that you do have the sort of courage needed to become a good witch."

"Really?" Cat glanced at Clara Bell.

"I have no doubt in my mind," Clara Bell said, smiling.

"Inner courage is what I'm talking about, Catherine," Ms. Roach continued. "The courage of not giving up. Of pursuing your magical dreams, regardless of how difficult that may be. Even though you are learning to control your fears, know that magic will always be a challenge for you." Cat nodded, and Ms. Roach went on. "I gather you are planning on reapplying to Ruthersfield next year—which is something no Late Bloomer has ever done before."

"I'd like to," Cat said.

A look of respect passed over the headmistress's face. "Then if you work on controlling your magic this year and don't do anything rash—like chasing after escaped criminals—and if you keep up your school grades as well as practicing your magical exercises . . ."

"Yes?" Cat whispered. She stood quite still, staring at the headmistress. Her heart was thumping so loud she could feel the blood rushing through her ears.

"If you do all that and you still want to come to Ruthersfield, then so long as you do well on the entrance exams, we would be delighted to offer you a place."

Cat burst into tears, something she was hugely ashamed of, but she couldn't help herself.

"Remember, Cat," Clara Bell said with a smile, as

Cat and her parents turned to go. "Believing in yourself and your magic is half the battle. You can do this, Cat Campbell. I know you can."

"I'm going to try my hardest," Cat said, taking her mum's and dad's hands. "And after facing Madeline Reynolds, I don't think anything can stop me now!"

Chapter Twenty-Six

. . . .

Dreams Do Come True

FOR THE NEXT TWELVE MONTHS CAT DID EVERYTHING Ms. Roach had asked her to do. Her father made her a beautiful model wand out of cherrywood so Cat could practice her wand techniques without worrying about her magic misfiring all over the bakery. He also helped her set up a terrarium for the pet tarantula Cat had requested on her birthday. She called the spider Maddie, and by the end of the year, Cat could pick Maddie up and let her crawl all over her hands without flinching.

The best part was that Poppy had agreed to help Cat study. Ms. Roach had given her permission, and even Uncle Tom didn't seem to mind. After all, it wasn't as if Poppy was actually performing the magic herself. She just gave Cat tips, and they spent two hours together every day practicing spells. Cat adored having her mother's help, but it was frustrating to see how easily witchcraft came to her, especially as Cat struggled so hard to channel her own inner magic.

"Focus on the pencil," Poppy instructed as Cat practiced rolling one across the kitchen table. She wanted to impress Ms. Roach at her next interview. "Channel your inner energy," Poppy said, remembering what she had been taught. "That way the magic can flow through." There were many moments when Cat felt like she would never master the basics, when she sent cupcakes and croissants rolling all over the bakery along with the pencil and her magic wouldn't do what it was supposed to do. But she refused to give up.

On Saturdays, after buying her walnut bread, Clara Bell would sit by the canal with Cat, discussing early magic in pagan times and the evolution of witchcraft through the ages. When Cat had trouble remembering important facts, Clara Bell taught her some useful tricks. "Fourteen four, fourteen four, wands were drawn on the Penine Moor," or "Twelve twenty-three, twelve twenty-three, Ruthersfield was founded by Witch Dupree." For Cat's birthday she gave her her own copy of *The Late Bloomer's Guide to Magic*, and Cat read a few lines every night for inspiration.

As autumn drifted into winter and winter melted into spring, Cat practiced and practiced until her head ached and her fingers were stiff from grasping her magic wand. Most evenings, Marie Claire tested Cat on her spell ingredients words, patiently correcting Cat every time she spelled "cowry shell" with a *k* instead of a *c*, or forgot how many *a*'s were in "sarsaparilla." And of course Cat's grandparents did everything they could to support their granddaughter, although it took Granny Edith a while to get over her disappointment when Cat didn't get offered a place at Ruthersfield straightaway. But on weekends, when Cat visited Pudding Lane, Granny Edith made up practice quizzes for her, and instead of playing cards they all sat around the kitchen table pretending to be on a game show. Grandpa Roger read out magic questions while Cat and her grandmother competed against each other for the correct answers. There were Twirlie bars for the winner, and plenty of laughter to keep Cat going.

As for Peter, he invented a device he liked to call "Cat's Adrenaline Beeper," which she kept in her pocket at all times. When Cat found herself getting worried or scared or even overexcited, the beeper would pick up her raised heartbeat and start buzzing, reminding her to stay calm and practice the deep-breathing techniques Francesca Fenwick was so keen on. At recess Cat would go along to science club with Peter and Adam. She liked to sit on the radiator and study spells while they did experiments and built things. Cat found she had much more in common with them these days than she did with Anika, who fainted when Cat introduced her to her new pet. Peter, on the other hand, was quite happy to let Maddie crawl all over his shoulders.

On the day of her Late Bloomer's exam, Cat was so nervous she was sure she wouldn't be able to remember a thing. It was a five-hour-long exam, both oral and written, with a special section devoted to the Passion Quiz. The written piece was fine. Cat knew most of the answers, but she had trouble with her potions. And even though she managed to roll a pencil nicely, she lost control halfway through and sent the pencil shooting across the room and out the window.

It took three weeks before the results came through. Every morning Cat met Ted Roberts, the postman, at the door, and he'd give his head a little shake. "Sorry, Cat, not today." When the long purple envelope with the Ruthersfield crest on the front finally arrived, Cat felt so nervous and her fingers were shaking so much, she could hardly open it.

"What if I failed?" Cat said, racing back with it into the kitchen. "What if they still don't want me?"

Her dad looked up from the map of Borneo he had spread across the table and saw the envelope in his daughter's hands. He gave his compass tattoo a rub for good luck, and said with complete confidence, "Course they will want you, Cat."

"There are no such things as failures," Marie Claire replied wisely. "Only steps toward success."

Cat stared at the letter in her hands.

"Well, go on, Cat," Poppy said, looking as anxious as Cat. "Aren't you going to open it?"

"I can't." Cat shook her head.

"Yes, you can," Poppy said.

It took all Cat's courage to rip open the envelope, and when she finally did, she let out a scream so loud it could be heard on the other side of the Ribbald Valley. "I got in!" Cat yelled, waving the paper in the air. "I'm going to Ruthersfield. Mamma, Dadda, Marie Claire!" She stared at the paper as if she couldn't believe it. "Ninety percent on the written test. Not so good in the practical though. I only got a C. But I aced the Passion Quiz." Cat thrust her arm in the air. "Maximum honors!"

"Oh, Cat, I'm so proud of you," Poppy said, overcome by a burst of emotion. "And I know your grandparents will be too!" She still found it hard to believe that this was what her daughter truly wanted.

"Gran's going to go nuts!" Cat said, dancing around the kitchen. "I can't wait to tell her."

Tristram beamed. "You earned this, Cat," he said.

"Cat, come here a moment," Poppy said, beckoning her daughter over. She held Cat by the shoulders and looked her right in the eye. "You know you're going to be the oldest student in the class, don't you? Probably by a good two or three years."

"Oh, I don't care about that, Mamma."

"And you'll always have to study three times as hard as everyone else. It's one of the most intense professions out there. Even girls who find magic easy struggle."

"Well, I'm used to studying. I've been working hard at my magic all year."

"I just want to make sure you really understand what you're getting yourself into, Cat."

Cat glanced at a tray of buns cooling on the table, waiting to be iced. *How could anyone choose baking over magic?* she thought. It made no sense to her at all. "I know what you're saying, Mamma, and I honestly don't care." Cat's eyes shone with happiness. "Of course I'm never going to be as good at magic as you or Great-Great-Granny Mabel. But I'll be doing what I love!" Cat said. "And that's all that really matters!"

The rest, as they say, is history. Cat started at Ruthersfield the following September, dressed in a smart new uniform with her own novice wand made of applewood. She oiled it every night to keep it supple, dabbing on her mother's extra special (and rather expensive) French walnut oil, which Poppy occasionally used in baking. It made the wood all shiny and smooth and gave it a delicious nutty smell. But after the first two terms, Poppy bought Cat a large bottle of bargain wand oil to take its place, saying rather firmly that this was what most witches used. Although Cat felt sure it didn't work quite as well.

Like Clara Bell, Cat never did master the art of potion making. But she refused to give up trying and could eventually turn out a respectable wart removal cream and an excellent memory-boosting tonic. Sadly, the more complex potions, like shape-changing brews and invisibility spells, would always be beyond her. Cat did manage to make Peter disappear one day, but she had trouble reversing the spell and it took two weeks for the magic to wear off. Poor Peter had to go around wearing a red woolly hat so everyone knew where he was, and after that he refused to let Cat practice on him again.

One thing Cat did excel at was broomstick flying, just like she always knew she would. In her second year at Ruthersfield she was asked to join the broomstick gymnastics team. There was nothing Cat liked better than swooping across the sky, and she got quite a reputation for her impressive stunts. She could balance on her broomstick standing up, and earned the school record for the most somersaults performed in mid-dive. As soon as she was old enough, Cat joined the meals on broomsticks program, and Clara Bell quickly promoted her to team leader because of her dedication and enthusiasm. Even on rainy days, Cat would put on her waterproof cloak and deliver hot meals to the elderly residents of Potts Bottom. And on special occasions, like May Day and Midwinter's Eve, Cat got her mother and Marie Claire to bake cookies for everyone, which she packed in pretty bags and flew around. By the time Cat was in year twelve, she had expanded the meals on broomsticks program and organized a weekly errand service, where girls picked up shopping lists and flew about town, collecting dry cleaning and cat food and delivering shoes to the cobblers. It was such a success that Cat earned a Community Service Award, which Poppy and

Tristram proudly hung in the bakery, next to Poppy's Young Baker of the Year awards.

When Cat graduated from Ruthersfield with respectable grades in most of her classes (although she did have to sit her potions exam three times before passing), and maximum honors in broomstick flying, she knew exactly what she wanted to do.

"I'm joining the Frequent Flyers," Cat told her parents, much to their pride and dismay. The Frequent Flyers were a group of witches trained to perform dangerous rescue missions, plucking people out of high-rise burning buildings or searching for survivors from boat accidents when the sea was too rough for the coast guards. They took their broomsticks to places it was impossible to reach otherwise and were known for their courage and bravery.

"I'm so proud of you!" Tristram said, his eyes a little damp with tears.

Poppy nodded in agreement, but she couldn't help saying, "Are you quite sure you want to be a Frequent Flyer, Cat? You're welcome to stay here and help out at the bakery."

"Absolutely, definitely not," Cat replied. "Just because I was born in a bakery doesn't mean I want to work in one." And, putting on her glare reflective, tinted flying goggles, she decided to take her graduation present—the streamlined 140 Speed Demon—up for a test spin. For old times' sake, Cat carried the broomstick up to her bedroom and climbed out onto the roof. She stood for a moment looking over the canal to the Ribbald Valley beyond. Then, with a cry of delight, Cat Campbell leapt off the bakery and launched herself into the air!

Excerpts from the Late Bloomer's Guide to Magic

by
Francesca Fenwick

....

Tips for the Late Bloomer

Congratulations on inheriting the magic gene! Witchcraft is a challenging profession, but it can also be extremely rewarding, even for the Late Bloomer. Below are a few pointers that I hope any Late Bloomers out there might find useful.

1. Believing in yourself and your magic is half the battle.
2. Pay attention to your breathing when you are mixing potions. Magical ingredients are sensitive to vibrations and can react badly with nervous energy.
3. Use a calm, deep voice when chanting your spells.
4. A positive attitude is just as important as being skillful with your wand.

5. Try not to give up if your spells don't work correctly the first time. It can take patience and a few tries to get the magic right.

6. Never compare your success to that of other witches. Be your own best self.

7. Try not to worry too much about the future. If you spend all your time fretting about your career as a witch (whether you'll ever be good enough, et cetera . . .), you'll miss out on all the wonderful magical moments going on right now!

8. Be proud of your Late Bloomer status. (If you are interested in joining the Society for Late Bloomers, please feel free to drop me a line. We are a small but growing organization.)

9. Most important of all—have fun with your magic. Keep your sense of humor at all times, and remember that laughter helps keep spells light and airy, which all good magic needs.

10. And finally, let us not forget what the great witch Annabelle Lewis said when she defeated the forces of evil: "Nem zentar topello"—Don't let fear stand in your way.

Simple Spells for the Late Bloomer

All these beginner spells are quite easy to control and are a good place for the novice witch to start. Ask an adult for permission and/or to help you to set up and use kitchen equipment, crack eggs, cut with knives, or take pans in and out of the oven, etc.

Raising Your Spirits Cake

Makes 1 cake or 12 cupcakes

When you are full of the grumps and life feels challeng-ing, make this delicious, light-as-air cake to lift your spirits. Be careful with your measurements and do *not* exceed 1 teaspoon of dragon's breath; otherwise the results may not be quite what you expected.

Don't worry if you can't track down any dragon's breath. Your cake will be just as delicious without it, and it should still raise your spirits if you say the chant-ing spell with an extra degree of enthusiasm.

~ INGREDIENTS ~

½ cup (1 stick) butter, softened

½ cup sugar

2 large eggs, at room temperature

4 ounces (just over ¾ cup) all-purpose flour

1 teaspoon baking powder

Pinch of salt

1 tablespoon milk

1 teaspoon condensed dragon's breath. (If you don't have
any dragon's breath, feel free to substitute 2 teaspoons of
vanilla extract. A tiny drop of red food coloring will give
the cake an authentic look because dragon's breath tints
the batter a lovely pale pink.)

~ Method ~

. . . .

1. Preheat the oven to 350° F.
2. Mix everything together in a food processor. Or use
   an electric beater to mix the butter and sugar together
   until light and fluffy, then add the eggs one at a time and
   beat well after each addition. Sift flour, baking powder,
   and salt together in a separate bowl and then mix into
   the batter until just blended. Add the milk and dragon's
   breath (or vanilla and food coloring if using).
3. Now hold a wooden (not metal) spoon in your left hand.
   Making sure you start in a clockwise direction, begin
   stirring the batter and in a clear, cheerful voice, chant
   the following spell:

Sunshine, moonbeams, light as air
Stir three times round without a care.
Warm winds, laughter, spirits rise
Stir back three times, counterclockwise.

4. Pour into a greased 7-inch cake pan or make as cupcakes. Bake cake for about 20 minutes (about 15 for cupcakes), until risen and springy to the touch. Cool on a wire rack.

5. If you like you can make a simple frosting for your cake by beating together 1 stick of softened butter, 1¼ cups of confectioners' sugar, and a teaspoon of vanilla extract. You will feel bubbles of happiness rising up inside you as you eat!

Amazing Dreams Bath Powder

Makes enough for several magical soaks

A long soak in this magical milky bath will give you amazing dreams. If you don't have any moon dust to add, don't worry. Just make sure you use a silky, sleepy voice when you say the chanting spell and you may still have wonderful dreams. A relaxing, sweet-scented bath is most certainly guaranteed.

~ INGREDIENTS ~

½ cup powdered milk

¼ cup cornstarch

Around 10 drops of lavender essential oil (less or more depending on how lavender scented you like it)

3 pinches moon dust

~ METHOD ~

1. Mix all the ingredients together with your wand. Stir in a clockwise direction and say the following chanting spell:

   A slice of moon
   A dash of wind
   A star to wish upon
   A magic world to fill your dreams
   And soon the night is gone.
   Weave enchantments through this spell
   And have amazing dreams to tell.

2. Keep your dream powder in a pretty sealed jar. Sprinkle a spoonful or two into warm running water for a magical bath experience.

Shortbread Giggle Bars

Makes about 35 Giggle Bars

Share this recipe with anyone in need of a good laugh. Giggling is not only encouraged but is necessary when you say the spell! These Giggle Bars may not produce quite such raucous chuckling without adding the pixie laugh to the batter, but they should certainly bring a smile to the face of the eater.

~ INGREDIENTS ~

1¼ cups all-purpose flour

½ cup plus 3 tablespoons cornstarch

¼ teaspoon kosher salt

⅓ cup plus 1 tablespoon sugar

1½ sticks (12 tablespoons) butter

A pixie laugh (The laugh of a pixie is very infectious, so be prepared to start giggling as soon as you let the laugh out of the bag. Feel free to substitute 2 teaspoons of vanilla extract if you can't track down any pixie laughs.)

~ METHOD ~

1. Preheat oven to 325° F.

2. Mix all the ingredients together in a food processor and pinch off a taste to make sure it's delicious. Now wave your wand over the dough and, with as much giggling as you can manage, chant the following spell:

   Silly jokes and lime green hair
   Teachers in their underwear.
   Random words at random times
   Funny songs and silly rhymes.
   Stir the pixie laugh in well
   And giggle while you say this spell!

3. Press the mixture into a 9 x 13 pan until it is in a thin, even layer. Score lightly into bars with a knife. Poke the dough all over with the prongs of a fork in a traditional shortbread design. (Shortbread was invented by Scottish pixies around the twelfth century.)

4. Bake for about 45 to 55 minutes, until pale golden. When the Giggle Bars come out of the oven, cut right through along the score lines and cool in pan on a wire rack. The shortbread will crisp as it cools. Sprinkle sugar over the bars and store in an airtight container at room temperature.

Songbird Lemonade

Makes 3 generous glasses of lemonade

Amaze and delight your friends, and sing like a nightingale after drinking this lemonade. You will hit the high notes, warble like an opera singer, and have flowers thrown at your feet. Nightingale calls are a specialty item. They can sometimes be ordered from *The Witches' Supply Catalogue*, but if you can't get hold of one, don't worry—just make the lemonade without it. By chanting the spell with a little extra chirpiness, you should still notice a difference in your singing voice, and of course, the lemonade will be just as delicious.

~ INGREDIENTS ~

½ cup sugar (or a little less, depending on how sweet you like
  your lemonade)

½ cup water

½ cup fresh lemon juice (you will need to squeeze about 3 to
  4 lemons depending on size and juiciness)

2 cups cold seltzer water

The call of a nightingale (Be careful when taking out of the
  box. Nightingale calls have a habit of flying off if you are

slow to grab them. Catch the call quickly as it comes out
of the box and drop straight into the lemonade.)

~ METHOD ~

. . . .

1. Heat the sugar and water together in a small saucepan
    until the sugar is dissolved completely. Take off the stove.
2. Put the sugar water into a pitcher. Add ½ cup of lemon
    juice. Then stir in 2 cups of seltzer water. Now, quickly
    add your nightingale call and wave your wand over the jug
    from right to left. In your best spell-chanting voice, sing:

Lemons and sugar and sparkling noise
Singing is one of life's marvelous joys.
The call of a cuckoo, the coo of a dove
The whistle of starlings from high up above.
A mocking jay sings with delight all day long
But the sweetest of all is the nightingale's song.
So mix in a melody, rhythm, and voice
Opera or rock and roll, make it your choice.
Blend it together and what have we made?
A musical potion of sweet lemonade.

3. Chill for 30 minutes. Pour into glasses and enjoy! You
    can serve this with ice or lemon slices if you would like.
    Remember to clink glasses and, before drinking, say the
    witches' toast to good health, "Daggles up!"

Courage Potion

When life feels overwhelming and a little scary (which is often the case for the Late Bloomer), this potion will give you the boost of courage you need. Drink a glass before school or broomstick flying or whatever else makes your insides quiver. If you have trouble finding powdered griffin's tooth to add to the potion, don't worry. This ingredient is extremely rare. Just make sure your voice doesn't quiver as you say the spell and there will still be plenty of courage in your potion.

~ INGREDIENTS ~

½ cup vanilla yogurt, or be courageous and try another flavor
¾ cup fresh or frozen fruit (Choose whatever kind you like.)
½ cup orange juice (Feel free to take control of your potion
    and pick a different juice.)
¼ cup ice cubes
1 teaspoon powdered griffin's tooth

~ METHOD ~

. . . .

1. Whiz all the ingredients together in a blender. Then wave
    your wand over the potion and using a calm, clear voice,
    say the following chanting spell:

    Courage is for lions
    Courage is for kings
    Courage is for all of us, scared of many things.
    We only need a little, a pinch to see us through
    So courage, courage, step right up
    Infuse our magic brew.

2. Pour into a glass and enjoy. You should feel yourself
    getting braver as you drink!

Friendship Repair Hot Chocolate

Makes 2 mugs of hot chocolate

This is the perfect brew for patching up quarrels and making friends again after an argument. Share a mug with the person you have been fighting with and watch those angry feelings melt away. Feel free to substitute regular whole milk if you don't have access to unicorn milk. The richer and creamier the milk, the better the hot chocolate will taste.

~ INGREDIENTS ~

. . . .

2 cups unicorn milk (or regular whole milk)
½ cup real chocolate chips
Fun stuff (Feel free to impress your friends by adding a drop
    of peppermint or vanilla extract, and if you really want to
    make them swoon, top with a cloud of whipped cream.)

~ Method ~

. . . .

1. Warm the milk in a saucepan over medium heat. Mix in chocolate chips and stir or whisk until melted. Turn off the heat and wave your wand over the pan. In your warmest, friendliest voice, chant the following spell:

A hug, hello, and friendly wink
Stir all these things into this drink.
Add smiles and laughs, a listening ear
To help your quarrel disappear.
So share a cup with friend or foe
And watch your friendship mend and grow.

2. Pour hot chocolate into mugs. Add the fun stuff if you want to, and make sure you clink cups with your friend before drinking, and say the witches' toast to good health, "Daggles up!"

Acknowledgments

M Y NAME MAY BE ON THE COVER OF THIS BOOK, BUT
I could not have written it without the help and
support of a great many people, starting with my wonderful agent, Ann Tobias. Once again she worked with
me through endless rounds of revisions, and *Cat* would
not be the book it is today without her excellent guid-
ance and help—thank you, thank you!

A huge thank-you to my dream editor, Paula
Wiseman, for helping me breathe magic into Cat, and
to everyone at Simon & Schuster who worked so hard
on this book, especially Chloë Foglia, for her fabulous
cover design.

Thank you to the amazingly talented Sebastien
Mesnard, for bringing Cat to life. He captured her
perfectly in his gorgeous illustration, and I feel so lucky
to have his artwork on my cover!

Where would I be without the sharp eagle eyes of Jane Gilbert Keith, who picks up things no one else ever notices and brainstorms ideas with me over countless cups of tea. I can't forget to mention Annalie Gilbert Keith and Juliette Lowe, who gave me excellent feedback from a kid's point of view.

Thank you to everyone who insisted I write a sequel to *Poppy*, and to my son Ben for giving me the brilliant idea! Thank you to my family and friends, for the constant encouragement and daily laughter. And to Rachel Roberts, for making sure all my spells worked correctly. I also want to say a special thank-you to the entire Lowe clan. I couldn't ask for a more wonderful bunch of in-laws!

I am so lucky to have such supportive parents, who read countless drafts of *Cat* and listened to me ramble away for hours on the telephone while I worked through plot ideas.

And lastly, thank you to my husband, Jon, for doing all the yucky chores and ferrying the kids about so that I could have time to write! And to Sebastian, Oliver, Ben, and Juliette—you inspire me to be more courageous every day.